Able Team's prisoner begged Carl Lyons to make a deal

"American, the others cannot hear. Listen to my offer. You could do very well for yourself. I pay in gold."

"I don't fight for money," Lyons said matter-of-factly.

"You risk your life for ideals? Don't be naive, that is for teenagers and charities. You could start at a thousand dollars a week if you join with me. Are you interested, American?"

Lyons opened a beer for his prisoner. He glanced over his shoulder at his partners across the room, then passed the beer to Gunther.

"I have my ideals."

"We all do. A thousand a week, in gold. A starting salary."

"Paid into a numbered account?"

"Automatically. Are you interested?"

Carl Lyons nodded.

Mack Bolan's
ABLE TEAM

Mack Bolan's
PHOENIX FORCE

ABLE TEAM
Into
the Maze

Dick Stivers

A GOLD EAGLE BOOK FROM
W🦅RLDWIDE

TORONTO • NEW YORK • LONDON • PARIS
AMSTERDAM • STOCKHOLM • HAMBURG
ATHENS • MILAN • TOKYO • SYDNEY

First edition October 1984

ISBN 0-373-61214-1

Special thanks and acknowledgment to
G.H. Frost for his contributions to this work.

Printed in Canada

1

Surrounded by death, the colonel lay in the dust, his hands tied behind his back, a rope around his neck. Flies found his open wounds and the blood clotting on his gray uniform. His North American and Yaqui captors stood in a circle around him, automatic rifles in their hands.

Black, choking smoke drifted from the wreckage of burning helicopter troopships. Here and there, the white fire of magnesium blazed in the hulks. Molten aluminum flowed from the wrecks. In the ashes, the aluminum puddled in shimmering iridescent mirrors.

A Mexican soldier dying of burns screamed until a single rifle shot silenced him. Only skeletons and charred meat remained of the other Mexican soldiers who had died in the explosions.

Minutes before, on this ridge in the desert wilderness of the Mexican state of Sonora, Able Team and a group of teenage Yaqui Indians had annihilated two squads of elite airborne commandos. Rosario Blancanales, the Puerto Rican ex-Green Beret, called The Politician by his fellow warriors, triggered set charges of explosives and kerosene to destroy the squads as they left their Bell UH-1 Huey troopships. On a hilltop to the east, ex-LAPD officer Carl Lyons faced a third Huey. Of the squad of soldiers in that troopship, only the colonel survived.

Carl Lyons asked the first question of the interrogation. "What's your name, Colonel?"

"Gunther. I'm Colonel Jon Gunther. I was assigned to help the Mexicans capture you."

"Who assigned you?"

"My commander, General Mendez."

"Where is your base?"

"To the west. There is a place called Rancho Cortez on the coast. It was used by Colonel Gonzalez as his base."

"Is General Mendez there?"

"No. The general issued his instructions by telephone."

"Where is General Mendez?"

"I don't know. He could have called from Culiacan."

"How many soldiers at the Rancho?"

"Hundreds. There are barracks. There is an airfield. There is—"

"Can you draw a map?"

"Yes."

Rotorthrob came from the east. Silhouetted against the rising sun, a Huey troopship flew in a slow circle over the ridges. The helicopter had been captured in an action the night before. Piloted by an agent from the United States Drug Enforcement Agency, the helicopter would carry Able Team and their allies to the next fight.

The hand-radios carried by Lyons and Blancanales buzzed.

"Looks like you did it to them," the voice of Gadgets Schwarz commented.

As the electronics specialist of Able Team, Gadgets had stayed with the captured helicopter and monitored the radio frequencies of the Mexican army units during the fighting.

"It's time to move," Gadgets told them. "The action's picking up. A flight of goons—"

Lyons spoke into his hand-radio to interrupt his partner. "Tell me later. We got a prisoner listening. Any radio calls to out here?"

"Their base called for a report. But no one answered, and they think that's strange. I think it's time to get out."

"Ready to go. There's nothing left here."

Rotor wind threw dust and ashes as the helicopter descended to the ridge. Inside, Gadgets Schwarz and Miguel Coral—a Mexican gang *pistolero* cooperating with the DEA and Able Team—sat on the troop bench with several radios. Coral slipped off his headphones and reached out to help Lyons and Blancanales with the prisoner. Lyons motioned Coral back to the radios.

"Stay on those radio frequencies," Lyons commanded. "That's more important. We'll load up."

Coral nodded. Only days before, Coral—with his wife and three of his young children, escorted by a truckful of gunmen—had attempted to escape from the drug wars of Northern Mexico by crossing into the United States. Able Team had teargassed his bodyguards, then captured Coral. To gain his freedom from prison and sanctuary for his family, Coral agreed to lead Able Team against Los Guerreros Blancos, a new heroin syndicate using military weapons and Mexican army troops to eliminate the other drug gangs, including the syndicate Coral had served for decades, the Ochoa Family.

Yaquis helped Lyons and Blancanales push the six-foot-five, two-hundred-twenty-pound Colonel Gunther through the door. Blancanales lashed the prisoner into a safety harness to prevent a suicide dive from the airborne troopship. Yaquis loaded M-60 machine guns and steel cans of ammunition into the helicopter.

Pete Davis, the DEA pilot, shouted to them, "Now back to the camouflage?"

Lyons nodded. "Conference time."

In seconds, the helicopter—overloaded with men and weapons and equipment—left the ridge line. Lyons looked back to see a line of Yaquis jogging down the mountainside. The group would join them later.

The helicopter veered to the north. In three directions, the vast panorama of the Sierra Madre Occidental extended to the horizon. To the west, the direction of the Pacific Ocean and the coastal cities, the mountains became foothills and desert plains. Distance and haze denied any sight of the coast.

Dropping below the ridge lines, the pilot followed a snaking canyon. Panicked birds shot from the mesquite and cactus as the thundering machine flashed past, the rotors throwing dust and leaves to swirl behind the helicopter. After a few kilometers, the helicopter descended to a sandy river bottom shaded by cottonwoods.

The rotors spun to a stop. Yaquis emerged from

the cottonwood dragging screens of lashed-together branches. They quickly covered the helicopter. The camouflage screens concealed the helicopter from airborne observation and shaded the OD-green troopship from the desert sun.

Lyons dumped Colonel Gunther onto the riverbed's sand. Then he turned to Gadgets and Coral. He asked them in a whisper, "What about the transmissions you monitored?"

"One was very interesting. It came in on this black box." Gadgets touched the radio designed and manufactured by United States National Security Agency. The Mexican army unit used the secure-frequency radio to communicate with their base. Similar to the hand-radios Able Team used, but with more frequencies and range, the radio employed encoding circuits to scramble every transmission, decode every message received. Without a matching radio, anyone scanning the bands would intercept only bursts of electronic noise.

"A planeful of goons came in from Mexico City. They wanted to report directly to Colonel Gunther. A Mexican army officer said Colonel Gonzalez commanded the operation. The goons said they'd radio their general in Mexico City for instructions. But then the Mexicans said Gunther was with Gonzalez and the goons went ahead and landed." Gadgets turned to Coral. "I get that right?"

Coral nodded. "The soldiers from Mexico City would not accept orders from Mexican army officers."

"Mexico City? That's where their general is?" Lyons asked.

"Yeah."

"Anything else?"

"Just calls to ones that got wasted."

"A general in Mexico City...." Lyons considered the information. He stepped from the helicopter.

Blancanales watched as Gunther sketched a map of Rancho Cortez. A Yaqui teenager named Ixto stood two steps back from Gunther, an FN FAL rifle pointed at the prisoner's head.

"The barracks." Colonel Gunther pointed to the line of rectangles he had drawn. "The administrative buildings, the landing field, the aircraft hangars. Fuel tanks. The building for the electric generators. The road to the dock. A rifle range. Here is the beach."

"And the perimeter?" Blancanales prompted.

"Outside, a barbed-wire cattle fence. Then a cleared area. Then an eight-foot chain link fence with concertina wire."

"That's the highway?" Blancanales pointed to the edge of the paper. "What's that other line?"

"A railroad connection. At one time the Rancho processed sugar cane for Mexico and the United States. That is why there is also a dock for ships."

"And what does it process now?" Lyons asked.

"That was fifty or sixty years ago," Colonel Gunther answered. "Now the Rancho is only for the army."

"There's no heroin labs there?"

"I did not see that."

"What army?"

"The army of Mexico."

Lyons pointed to the gray fatigues and black web

gear and boots Gunther wore. At his collar, a silver eagle clutching lightning bolts in its claws identified Gunther as a colonel. "You're not wearing a Mexican uniform. Who hired you?"

"General Mendez."

"General Mendez of the International?"

"That is what they call themselves."

"Who are they?"

"The International? I don't know. Rich men. I know only General Mendez. He paid me. He issued instructions. I know only him."

"Where is he?"

"I don't know."

"How do you contact him?"

"I don't. He called me."

"Is he in Culiacan?"

"I don't know."

"Where is the base in Culiacan?"

"There is no base in Culiacan. There is only the Rancho, near Obregon."

"Where are you based?"

"At the Rancho—"

"Before the Rancho?"

"In New York and Washington. The capital of your country."

"Where are the bases?"

"I don't know. We worked in hotels."

"This general lives in hotels?"

"The general never took me to his home."

"The International does business from hotels?"

"For security. They rent conference rooms for the meetings. Then no one needs to go outside the hotel during the meetings."

"Where are you from?"

"I was born in Paraguay."

"You look German."

"My family came from Germany."

"Before the war or after?"

"At the beginning of the century. Before the First World War."

"How many soldiers at that base?" Lyons pointed to the map of Rancho Cortez.

"I saw hundreds. I don't know the number."

"He's telling you nothing!" Standing beside Lyons, a young man from Tucson, Arizona, known by the Chicano name of Vato, stared down at Gunther. This leader of the Yaqui warriors had proven himself a relentless, merciless enemy of Los Guerreros Blancos in his fight beside Able Team. "Let us question him—"

"No. We need him alive."

"He may die," Vato admitted. "But he will answer our questions."

"Tie him," Lyons told the Yaquis guarding the colonel. "His hands, his elbows, his feet. I don't want him trying to escape. He's too valuable to kill."

Lyons motioned to his partners. "Vato, too. And you, pilot. Outside. Bring that map."

Thrashing through tangled branches, they followed him away from the camouflaged helicopter. They crossed the stream bed to the shade of the cottonwoods. Lyons scanned the sky for spotter planes. He saw only a hawk soaring in the infinite blue of the sky above the canyon.

Gadgets ran through the sand to Lyons. "We ain't hitting that base. No way. So don't even talk about it."

"I remember Honduras," Lyons told his partner. "No more banzai attacks."

"You just keep remembering. I still don't know how we lived through it back then. That night was extreme-ly insane!"

They sat on the bank of the dry stream. The arching branches of the cottonwoods screened them from airborne observation. Cicadas whined behind them, the rising and falling noise of the desert grasshoppers the only sound in the stillness of the narrow canyon.

"Do you believe what he said?" Blancanales asked.

Lyons shook his head. "He's lying."

"I don't think he's lying about the base." Blancanales held up the map of Rancho Cortez. "Look at the details. Who would imagine an army base would have a dock for freighters?"

"He wants us to hit that base." Lyons took the map and studied it. "Maybe he thinks we'll try to infiltrate. Use him to get inside—"

"No!" Gadgets interrupted. "You try any shit trick like that, you're going alone."

"Not smart, Ironman." Blancanales shook his head at the thought of an assault on the Mexican army installation.

Vato spoke. "In three days, I could gather fifty men and women with rifles."

Miguel Coral nodded. "I have many friends in Sonora and Sinaloa. We could gather all those who hate—"

"No!" Gadgets cut the discussion. "No talk. No plans. I don't even want to think about it."

Lyons looked to the group of men. "Notice he

didn't say anything about Mexico City? Nothing at all. Not a word.''

"He talked about New York and Washington," Blancanales said.

"But nothing about Mexico City," Lyons insisted. "A gang of millionaire fascists, with private armies everywhere in Central and South America, starts a billion-dollar-a-month heroin operation in Mexico. They wipe out or take over the Mexican drug gangs. They set up their own military base. They use corrupt politicians and corrupt army officers. An emergency comes along and they've got help flying in from Mexico City the next day. But our prisoner tells us the leaders run the operation from New York and Washington. Maybe if he'd said Miami, I'd almost believe him. But he didn't.''

"Mexico City is big," Blancanales cautioned. "The biggest city in the world. I doubt if the offices of the Fascist International will be listed in the phone book.''

"This is it.'' Lyons pointed to the map of Rancho Cortez. We can go up against this army base—''

"No!" Gadgets interrupted again.

Lyons continued. "Hundreds of soldiers, reinforcements arriving all the time, a double security perimeter with all kinds of surprises, helicopters, planes, heavy weapons, napalm. . . .''

"I think he's seen the light," Gadgets marveled. "Ironman thinks, Ironman reasons. I don't believe it— Ahggh—''

Lyons caught his partner in a headlock to silence his sarcasm. While Gadgets struggled against the hold, Lyons continued. "Or we can fly down to Mexico City. Make like tourists and maybe hit them where they'd never expect.''

Breaking Lyons's hold, Gadgets gasped, ''Second the motion.''

''Could we take the helicopter that far?'' Lyons asked Davis.

''Twelve or thirteen hundred miles? And without maintenance? Might make it. We'd need at least four refuelings.''

''What do you think, Vato?'' Lyons asked the Yaqui leader.

''Exploit confusion. Move secretly. Strike where unexpected.''

Lyons nodded. ''Will you come with us?''

''If we cut off the head, the body will die,'' Vato answered. ''I will go. Perhaps a few of the others.''

Lyons turned to Coral. ''And you, Miguel?''

''You give me the opportunity to kill those who murdered my friends, who murdered the son of my *patrón*? I thank you for the opportunity.''

''Then it's unanimous,'' Blancanales concluded. ''We go to Mexico City.''

COLONEL GUNTHER LAY IN THE SAND, immobilized by ropes, guarded by teenagers with automatic rifles, his mind calculating how he could survive. His intelligence had already saved his life once that day.

Suspecting an ambush, Gunther had directed his helicopter pilot to land on another hilltop. But the petty-pompous Mexican officer commanding the other two troopships of Mexican airborne soldiers disregarded Gunther's suspicions. The Mexican commander took his men and helicopters blindly into the killzone.

But bad luck also condemned Colonel Gunther and his squad of soldiers. As explosions and waves of flame decimated the Mexicans, a second group of North Americans and Yaquis struck. Gunther lost his soldiers, his pilots, his UH-1 troopship.

Now, a prisoner of a group of North Americans and Yaqui campesinos wearing stolen army of Mexico uniforms, Gunther faced interrogation by torture, then death.

Gunther put his thoughts beyond the fear of death. Fear could not save him. Only his intelligence and experience could gain him the time he needed.

When the Americans had questioned him, he answered their questions. He drew the map of the Rancho. He had even revealed details about the operations of the International in the United States. The answers had gained time.

Time for thought. Time for cunning.

And if, in ignorance or overconfidence, the North Americans attempted to use Gunther or his information in their assault against the International. . . .

Then he would reverse this defeat. He would regain his freedom.

And they would die.

2

Below them, the shadow of the troopship skipped over hills and desert, the silhouette of the fuselage circled by the shadow of the spinning rotors. The shadow flashed over pale, windblown sand and colorless earth. Sometimes the shadow disappeared when the helicopter passed over canyons, the shadow lost within shadows for an instant. Once they passed over a road, but they saw no trucks, no farms, no villages.

Four Yaquis—Vato, Ixto, Jacom and Kino—sat in the doors, their feet dangling into space, a rope across the door serving as a safety restraint. They pointed out landmarks to one another as they passed over the familiar territory. Behind them, Able Team struggled to read a map as the slipwind from the open doors flapped and tore the map. Colonel Gunther—tied, blindfolded, wads of rags taped over his ears—sat in a doorgunner's seat, the safety harness buckled around him.

Blancanales held a compass out at arm's distance, away from the metal of the bulkheads. He watched the needle, then looked down to the shadow of the helicopter to confirm the bearing. He shouted to his partners.

"Davis is taking us due south. Wasn't the plan to stay away from the coast?"

"That's where the army is." Lyons spoke into the intercom microphone. "Davis, where you going?"

"I'm paralleling the mountains."

"Our compass tells us you're going straight south."

"Got to, for a while."

"Got to, nothing! You run us into the army, we'll never make it to Mexico City."

"Hey, specialist, I'm the pilot. You see those mountains to the east? The charts say those mountains go up to eleven and twelve thousand feet. If this aircraft were empty, I couldn't get in higher than ten thousand feet. And we're overweight. That means we stay low in the foothills."

"Yeah? If the Mexicans pick us up on radar, they're going to wonder who we are. And that could lead to very serious problems."

"Don't worry about the radar," Davis countered. "Worry about the questions when we refuel. A gang of Indians and gringos shows up in an army of Mexico helicopter and asks for a fill-up?"

"They're all in Mexican uniforms."

"What about you?"

"No problem. We're tourists. The army's taking us sight-seeing."

"Uh-huh."

Lyons turned to his partners and shouted, "He says we're overloaded and he can't get the altitude to stay in the mountains."

Blancanales spoke into the intercom. "Any way we can lighten the helicopter?"

"Throw out the prisoner," Davis answered.

"We need him—"

"Then jump out yourself."

"No, thanks."

"Then instead of asking me questions, do something. Try unbolting the cargo doors and dropping them."

"That'll have to wait until we land."

"Then get together with all those passengers back there and work out a way we can onload two hundred gallons of filtered, unadulterated Jet A kerosene without any questions asked."

"*¡Avión!*" Jacom yelled.

"*¿Dónde?*" Coral yelled back.

The Yaquis in the right-hand door pointed to a glint of light in the west. Lyons scanned the sky with his binoculars and pointed to another speck.

"A light plane and a helicopter," he said.

Blancanales relayed the information to Davis. "We got a helicopter and a spotter plane to the west-southwest."

The troopship dropped. Lyons and Blancanales grabbed the safety rope across the door as Davis took the troopship down. The skids seemed to touch the ridge lines.

Davis shouted through the intercom, "Get on their frequencies. Listen for an alert—"

Gadgets interrupted. "Already on it, fly-boy. Me and Señor Coral have been on it nonstop, all day long."

"What're they saying now?" Davis asked.

Gadgets laughed. "What they've been saying all day. 'Co-lon-el Gonzalez, where are you?' The helicopter and plane are on the way to look for their little lost colonel."

Lyons took the intercom microphone. "Just make distance, Davis. Get us out of here before they get serious."

As Sergeant Castillo banked the Piper in a slow circle of the destroyed helicopters, Lieutenant Lopez focused his binoculars on the scene. He saw the ashes and blackened metal that had been four helicopters. Knots of vultures fought over the corpses of dead soldiers.

The lieutenant spoke into the radio. "We are above the hill. I count four helicopters. They are burned, nothing left. There is no one alive down there."

After a moment, questions came from the radio. "This is Colonel Alvarez. You see only four helicopters?"

Lieutenant Colonel Alvarez, the International Group's second-in-command, directed the search for the missing Colonel Gonzalez from the safety of the communications office of Rancho Cortez.

"Only four."

"Is there evidence of fighting?"

The lieutenant exchanged glances with the sergeant. The sergeant shook his head at the question. Suppressing a laugh, the lieutenant answered, "Yes."

"Continue searching. We must determine the whereabouts of the other helicopters and the bomber plane."

The sergeant pointed to a scorched hillside. Straightening the Piper's flight path, he crossed the narrow canyon, then circled again. Below them, they saw a tangle of heat-distorted scrap metal. Burning fuel had denuded the hillside, leaving only ashes and black rocks. A rotor blade identified the wreck as that of a helicopter.

On a hilltop above the wreck, vultures fed on the bodies of soldiers in gray uniforms. Two corpses lay on the top of the hill. Others sprawled in the brush on the steep hillside. Vultures had found them all.

Studying the hilltop through the binoculars, the lieutenant saw no weapons. He reported his observations to Colonel Alvarez.

"We see another helicopter. And the bodies of the advisers from Mexico City. All dead. And their rifles and equipment are gone."

"They are dead? Incredible. I cannot believe they fell into a trap also."

"It is very strange. It is as if they were ambushed. But they died on a hilltop. Ambush would have been impossible."

"They are highly trained, veterans of many wars."

"But someone killed them all."

"Find the others," commanded the voice from the radio. "Perhaps Colonel Gonzalez escaped somehow. Perhaps the pilot of the plane survived. We must learn exactly what happened. Has the helicopter carrying the soldiers arrived yet?"

"In a few minutes, Colonel."

"They will search the area. Assist them."

The lieutenant switched off the microphone. He said to the sergeant, "We will assist them. We will tell them to stay away from this cursed place. And perhaps they will live."

LANDING IN AN ARROYO outside Culiacan, Davis switched off the turbine. He turned to his passengers.

"We still got some fuel, but not much," he said. "How about if we get volunteers to hitchhike over to the airport? There's a dirt road a couple hundred yards that way—"

Davis pointed to the south. In the afternoon glare, the men of Able Team saw only heat-shimmering desert.

"How far to Culiacan?" Lyons asked.

"I guess we're about five miles outside city limits," Davis replied. "You can catch a bus on the highway."

"I have friends in the city," Miguel Coral told the North Americans. "I will go. Who will go with me?"

"We have no clothes, only uniforms," Vato answered, pointing to the camouflage-patterned Mexican army fatigues he and the three other Yaqui fighters wore.

"I can't," Gadgets answered. "I have to stay with the radios. And if you're going, the Politician's got to stay here to translate. So that means the Ironman goes. You still got your civilian clothes?"

Lyons pulled his wadded slacks and shirt from his pack. He found his sport shirt. As he dressed, Vato and the Yaquis spread out into the desert around the helicopter. In their uniforms, with Mexican army boots and gear and weapons, they looked like young soldiers on maneuvers.

"How much money you got?" Lyons asked Gadgets.

Gadgets took a plastic box from his pack. The stenciled word *Money* marked the lid. He took out stacks of crisp greenbacks in bank wrappers. "Ten thousand...twenty thousand...thirty thousand total. How much will two hundred gallons of kerosene cost?"

Davis stared at the money. "You always carry that much cash around in your backpack?"

"Nothing like pictures of Benjamin Franklin to expedite solutions to difficult situations," Gadgets jived as he counted out ten one-hundred-dollar bills. "Will a thousand dollars cover a fill-up?"

"Make it two thousand." Lyons buttoned up his sport shirt.

Gadgets laughed at Lyons's wrinkled, dirty clothes. "Look at that dude. He's so mean he even wipes out Perma-Press. Here's a thousand more. Buy yourself a new shirt."

"Yeah, yeah. You think you're funny. What if I take this money and buy an air ticket back to L.A.?"

"You won't do that."

"Why not?"

"Because the goons you want to kill ain't in L.A., that's why."

"You got it. *Adios, amigos.*"

Lyons and Coral hiked out of the arroyo. In the distance, across the rolling desert, they saw a gray smear: the smoke and auto pollution of Culiacan. Lyons checked his watch.

"Four o'clock. Think we can walk into town before night?"

"We will be there very soon. We could be done before night, but it is probably better that we come back with the truck after dark. To avoid questions."

They followed the dirt road toward the highway.

As they walked, Coral tutored Lyons in basic Spanish. The Mexican gangster taught the North American justice warrior numbers and directions and distances. He taught him nouns and the present tense of common verbs.

After a half hour's walking, they came to a sprawling dump. Plastic bags and broken glass littered the sand. Along the road, several families lived in *jacals*—shacks made of discarded sheet metal and plywood. Teenage boys looked up from sorting scrap metal and saw the two strangers. Children watched from the doorways of the shacks.

Coral called out to the teenagers. A boy pointed. A young man wearing oil-stained coveralls walked out to the strangers. He talked with Coral for a minute. Coral turned to Lyons.

"We can hire him to take us into Culiacan," he said.

"Sure," Lyons said.

Coral negotiated the price and then the young man left.

"I told him our truck broke down in the mountains, and we're going in for some parts. He wanted to repair the truck, but I told him it was a new American truck with computerized ignition and that's what went wrong."

A battered Chevy pickup, assembled of mismatched body panels, rattled out. Lyons saw packing cases in the cargo bed. Each box contained different metals: aluminum, copper, brass, iron. A chicken fluttered about, finally flying off the truck.

Coral sat in the center, Lyons against the passenger

door. The teenager leaned across the seat and introduced himself to his riders.

"Alejandro," he said.

"Carl." Lyons gave only his first name.

"Miguel."

Then Alejandro accelerated the truck down the dirt road. It shook, the springs squeaking. Bumping and lurching on the seat, Lyons tried to follow the conversation between the teenager and Coral. Failing to understand the Mexicans, he stared out at the passing desert. Soon they turned onto the highway.

Alejandro instructed Lyons in Spanish dialect during the ride. Lyons understood nothing. Finally, Coral interrupted the lesson to give Alejandro directions. Alejandro left the highway and drove through the suburbs of Culiacan.

Late-afternoon sunlight blazed from the turquoise, pink, aqua-blue colors of the stucco houses. American and European compact cars filled the driveways. Cinder-block walls topped with jagged broken glass divided the lots. Coral motioned Alejandro to stop.

Coral scanned the neighborhood. Lyons started to open the door. Coral caught his arm.

"Wait. Something is not right."

"What?"

"No children. There should be children." Coral spoke quickly with Alejandro. The teenager shook his head. Coral turned to Lyons again. "There is no festival, no parades today. There should be children in the street and the yards."

They waited. Coral spoke again with Alejandro. The teenager started up the truck. They drove through the neighborhood, scanning the parked cars. After a few minutes of driving through the streets, circling the blocks, they parked again. Coral went into a house.

"*¿Qué es la problema?*" Alejandro asked Lyons.

"*No sé.*" Lyons shrugged.

Tires squealed. An engine roared as a four-door sedan spun around the corner. Lyons saw the forms of men in the front and back seats. Then he saw the muzzle of a weapon come out of the side window.

Grabbing Alejandro, Lyons threw open the pickup's door.

3

Tires screamed as the sedan skidded to a stop. The fender and a headlight of the car crumpled as they slammed into the pickup. Flat on his belly beside the pickup, Lyons pulled his Colt Python from the hideaway holster at the small of his back.

A Mexican with slicked-back hair and gray polyester business suit ran in front of him, a sawed-off shotgun in his hands.

Lyons fired a 158-grain jacketed, X-headed hollowpoint into the Mexican's face. The slug smashed through flesh and skull, the expanding hollowpoint disintegrating, the fragments continuing through the gunman's brain to explode from the back of his head. The impact threw him down, already dead, his skull a bloody void.

Looking under the pickup, Lyons saw shoes and slacks running from the sedan. The mirror-polished shoes ran around the rear of the pickup. Lyons spun and fired as another gunman appeared, the hollowpoint catching the Mexican just above his open collar and tearing through his throat to sever the spine. Momentum carried the dying man forward, the last spasms of his heart pumping blood from the entry and exit wounds. He fell, his Uzi still gripped in his hands, a broken neck allowing his head to twist impossibly, his open, blind eyes staring up at the sky.

Another weapon popped, slugs punching through sheet steel, glass shattering. Lyons heard ricochets hum overhead. A window in a house broke. Someone screamed. Lyons looked back to Alejandro, saw the teenager staring around, his eyes wide with panic. He couldn't think of the Spanish words to calm the teenager so he shouted, "Be cool, be cool—everything'll be okay."

The sedan's engine roared again, the wheels spinning. A door slammed. As tire smoke clouded into the air, Lyons scrambled to the bumper of the pickup.

He saw the sedan's driver leaning low over the steering wheel. The engine whined at maximum rpm, but the sedan did not move, the spinning tires only smoking on the asphalt.

A gunman leaned from the front passenger-side window and sprayed a burst from an M-16, the high-velocity 5.56mm slugs shrieking into the house, shattering glass, ricocheting wildly from concrete.

The tires gained traction. Lyons sprinted as the sedan started away. From an arm's distance, he double-actioned slugs through the driver's-side window, a hollowpoint ripping away the side of the man's skull, a second shot punching through his dead hand and shattering the steering wheel, a third bullet spider-shattering the windshield.

Driven by a dead man, the sedan careened out of control. It sideswiped a parked Volkswagen, throwing the Volkswagen onto the sidewalk, the sedan continuing sideways, tires smoking, to hit another parked car.

The sedan flipped, scraping across the asphalt on its roof.

Lyons ran to the wrecked, bullet-pocked sedan. One gunman still lived. Struggling to push the driver's corpse away, he didn't see Lyons. Lyons kicked the gunman in the side of the head. The man cursed and tried to turn to face his attacker, the M-16 rifle in his hand. Lyons kicked him again.

Stunned, the gunman did not resist as Lyons dragged him out. Slinging the M-16 over his shoulder, Able Team's Ironman dragged the semiconscious gunman back to the pickup.

Coral and a middle-aged man ran from the house. The man held a folding-stock M-1 carbine. Lyons dumped the prisoner in the driveway, then ran to Alejandro.

"¿Usted bien?" Lyons asked the young man.

Alejandro put up his hands. *"Por favor, señor Norteamericano. No veo nada. No sé nada. Por favor, tengo dos niños, tengo una familia—"*

Lyons holstered his Python. He went to one knee beside the panicked Mexican. He took out a hundred-dollar bill and pressed it into the teenager's hand. Struggling with the Spanish words, he told him, *"Por usted. Gracias. Vaya. Vaya pronto.* Get out of here."

"Sí, señor Norteamericano. I go, okay! Shit, man, I go."

Alejandro jumped into his pickup. Grinding the gears, he accelerated away, driving over the body of the first gunman Lyons had killed.

Pausing to gather the weapons from the dead men, Lyons found a new Mini-Uzi gripped in the hands of the throat-shot gunman. He took the time to find the spare magazines in the dead man's pockets. A Mini-Uzi had all the features of a standard Uzi, with the addition of a superior folding stock and a 1200-rounds-per-minute rate of fire. He would not leave it for the local police to claim.

Heavy with weapons, Lyons crossed the street to Coral, who held the side door of a panel van open. Lyons threw the collection of weapons inside and climbed in.

The surviving gunman bled from a bullet wound and from two cuts the shape of the toe of Lyons's shoe. Lyons pulled the gunman's jacket down over his arms. Searching the semiconscious man quickly, he found a .38-caliber Smith & Wesson revolver in an ankle holster.

Coral got into the front seat and shouted, *"¡Juan! ¡Immediatamente!"*

His middle-aged friend threw a bandolier of magazines for the M-1 carbine into the panel van and started the engine. Slamming the van into gear, he whipped backward out of the driveway, then raced away.

Lyons found the gunman's wallet. He saw a badge and an identification card with the seal of the Republic of Mexico. The card bore the words: Director General de la Policia de Transito.

"What is going on?" Lyons asked as he passed the wallet forward to Coral. Coral glanced at the identification, then showed the badge and card to Juan.

"Sorry to involve you in our war," Juan told his visitors. "My son killed a Guerrero. So the *Federales* want to take revenge. You should have called, Miguel. I would have told you to visit another time."

"You mean, the White Warriors—Guerreros Blancos?" Lyons asked. He pulled out the gunman's belt and bound his hands behind his back.

"I do not mean a soldier. But they are with Los Guerreros, yes."

"And the *Federales*?" Lyons asked.

"They are all together. Culiacan is their city."

"Miguel, what about the fuel? We've got to get out of here."

"It is already arranged. That's why we went to Juan. He took care of our planes, before the war."

"Then let's get that fuel and get gone."

"A car follows!" Juan shouted.

Looking through the back windows, Lyons saw a new four-wheel-drive pickup closing on them. A man in a sports coat leaned from the passenger window. A submachine gun flashed.

Bullets hammered the van. Tempered glass sprayed the interior. The van swerved, throwing Lyons against the side. Another slug punched through the sheet metal.

Snatching up the sawed-off shotgun—a Remington 870 with a pistol-grip, the barrel cut back to fourteen inches—Lyons crawled to the shattered windows of the van's back doors. He looked out and saw the 4x4 truck drawing up parallel with the van.

The gunman in the 4x4 sprayed slugs at Juan. Lyons pressed down the Remington's safety and fired.

As the abbreviated shotgun rocked in his hands, Lyons pumped the slide and fired again.

He pumped the weapon and pulled the trigger a third time, but the hammer only clicked.

Impact slammed the van sideways. The swerving and sliding threw Lyons hard against the wall of the van again. Lyons looked forward and saw that the passenger door had flown open as the two vehicles banged into each other. He saw the unconscious gunman fall out. Scrambling for the door handle, Lyons saved the Mini-Uzi, then drew the door closed as the 4x4 truck hit their van again.

Juan stood on the brakes. The 4x4 continued on. Lyons looked at it through the shattered windshield and saw a gunman in the back clutching at the roll bar. No one drove the 4x4 now. The shotgun blasts had broken the windows, and they could see that the interior was sprayed with blood. As Lyons snapped out the steel folding stock of the Mini-Uzi, the truck smashed into a parked car. The impact launched the gunman over the cab and into the boulevard's traffic.

Juan swerved. The wheels of his van bumped over the gunman. The middle-aged gangster gave a ranchero yell. "Ayeeee-ha!"

"Everyone okay?" Lyons called out.

Laughing, Juan glanced back. He laughed and talked as he raced through traffic. "I like you, *rubio*. For a month now, we have hidden in the house and said we were neutral, we were out of it, we wanted no trouble. Now we must move to another city, but in five minutes we killed six! Where is the other one?"

"He fell out."

"Seven we killed! They will respect this old man!"

TWO HOURS LATER, with the sun setting behind them,they bumped over the dirt road in a flatbed truck. Lyons rode with his feet on two cases of cold Dos Equis beer. Both Lyons and Coral held cardboard boxes full of roast chickens, tortillas, corn on the cob, plates of refried beans, chilis and chocolate cookies.

As Juan drove, he and Coral exchanged stories, sometimes in English, usually in Spanish. Lyons unwrapped the plastic around a kilo of hot tortillas and stuffed one in his mouth. He took another one, scooped up some refried beans. He ate tortillas and beans and watched the shacks pass.

As they arrived at the junkyard *jacal* where Alejandro lived with his family, they saw lanterns and people dancing in the warm evening to the blaring disco music of a transistor radio. A pink-and-blue Mickey Mouse *piñata* hung on a wire, ready to be destroyed by the children. Alejandro sat at the head of a table, pouring tequila for a group of friends. They listened as he told a story. He pointed with his index fingers—like a two-gun *pistolero*—to dramatize moments.

Coral looked at Lyons. They laughed.

They directed Juan to the arroyo where the others had camouflaged the helicopter. Juan took the flatbed truck, with its four fifty-five-gallon barrels of jet fuel on the back, to the edge of the hiding place. From there a hose would siphon the fuel into the troopship's tanks.

Lyons shouted to his partners and the Yaquis. "Party time!"

"What's the occasion?" Gadgets questioned from the darkness of the arroyo.

"For a start," Lyons muttered, "we lived through another day."

4

Bandages covered the right side of the agent's face. A plaster cast immobilized his right shoulder and arm. Outside the window of the private room, birds fluttered in the courtyard of the clinic. The only survivor of the two surveillance units, Agent Nava, now sedated against terrible pain, described the killer of the other federal officers.

"A North American. Blond, but dark from the sun. Tall, I think. Strong. A very good shot. He killed the others with only a pistol."

Sitting beside the agent's hospital bed, Captain Gomez noted the details on a pad. He underlined the words "North American." "Did he speak Spanish or English?"

"English only. When I rode in the van, I pretended to be unconscious. I listened to what they said. They talked in English about the White Warriors and—"

"The American did?"

"Yes, he knew of us. They talked of the Warriors and the federals and the army. The ones in the front, I don't know who said what, but they talked of the organization. Then they talked about 'the fuel.'"

"Gasoline?"

"No, they used the word 'fuel.' One of them, the

Mexican, said, 'That's why we went to Juan. He took care of our planes.' That is what they said."

"Then they were Ochoas?"

"They never said 'Ochoa.' But I think the Mexican was an Ochoa. He said 'our planes.' That is what Juan Perez did for the Ochoa Gang, right?"

Captain Gomez nodded. "The Mexican and Perez were Ochoas, but not the American. Interesting. They said they needed the fuel for their plane?"

"No. They never said what. Not a plane, not a truck, not a boat. They only said, 'fuel.' What happened to that Perez? Have you killed him yet?"

"No, he and his family escaped. We are searching—we alerted our units in the north—but nothing yet. Maybe Perez went with the others. We will learn soon. We have alerted all our men in the other cities."

"Kill him. We should have killed him weeks ago. When his son killed our man."

"We thought we could use him. But now he dies. And those others."

Folding his note pad closed, Captain Gomez left the ward. His driver took him directly to his next appointment. The driver parked the car and went into a downtown office. After a wait of a few minutes, an officer of the United States Drug Enforcement Agency got in the car.

The driver wove through the city traffic while the officials in the back seat discussed the events of the previous day. The Texas-born DEA agent laughed when he heard the description of the American gangster who had killed the *Federales*.

"Well, where'd that fellow come from?" he said

with a chuckle. "He's supposed to be dead. We had him shot down."

"Who?" Captain Gomez asked, confused by the Texan's response.

"That's Carl Lyons. He's called The Ironman because he's into weapons. He and his partners volunteered to work with the agency, and the agency sent him south to work with us. Damn, we couldn't have that. So we had their plane shot down. We were told it crashed and burned, no survivors. Damn, this complicates everything."

"What do you mean?"

"They're going to know who set them up! We sent them out there to fly over what we told them was a Mexican army operation. And the Mexicans shot them down. That puts us and the army on their shit list. And then yesterday this Lyons fellow shoots it out with *Federales*. That means they go it alone from now on. They won't trust anyone. Makes it more difficult to kill them."

"Who are these men?"

"Hotshots. Specialists. Antiterrorist terrorists. Always interfering in our operations. Thought we'd get rid of them this time."

"But they are still alive."

"Yeah, and while they're alive, there won't be no end to the trouble. So we got to fix that." The Texan looked directly at Captain Gomez. "We'll work close on it with you, okay? For our mutual benefit."

Returning to the federal offices, Captain Gomez typed up a summary of the information. One copy went by courier to Rancho Cortez. And one copy went by coded transmission to Mexico City, to the offices of the International.

BELOW THE HELICOPTER, the land became lush, tropical. Groves of bananas and avocados spread across mountains. Red dirt roads cut through jungles. As they neared Tepic, the sky darkened with the rain clouds of a southern storm.

Blancanales saw railroad tracks. He matched the landmarks and the railroad line to a map, then spoke into the intercom.

"You see the airport?"

"I've got it on the radio," Davis answered.

"How's the fuel?"

"Getting low. But the airport's coming up."

Turning to his partners, Blancanales saw Gadgets sleeping. Lyons and Coral studied the land under them. Coral pointed to a grove of trees. Clearings appeared here and there in the trees. A paved road cut past the groves.

Lyons shouted to Blancanales, "How far?"

"Close."

"Look there." Lyons pointed to the grove.

"Yeah, but Davis wants to get closer to the airport."

Lyons nodded. The helicopter banked. To the east, they saw the hangars and runways of the airport. A few kilometers to the south, sunlight flashed from the windows and sheet-metal roofs of thousands of houses and shops. Then the storm clouds moved across Tepic. A smear of rain trailed from the clouds.

"How close are you going to the city?" Blancanales asked Davis.

"I'm circling for a spot now. See a good place?"

"In those trees."

A tight bank took them back to the grove. Davis eased the troopship into a clearing. The rotor tips thrashed the nearest trees, chopping leaves and branches, then the skids touched the red earth and Davis switched off the power.

Silence.

Their ears rang in the sudden absence of turbine whine. Vato and the three Yaqui teenagers left the helicopter and took guard positions, playing the role of soldiers.

Gadgets woke and stared around him. "Where are we?"

"Tepic," Coral answered.

"Where's that?"

"Eight hundred kilometers from Mexico City."

The afternoon light went gray, and rain swept the grove with a sound like a wave breaking. The downpour bowed the trees' branches and hammered the aluminum of the troopship. In seconds, pools of water covered the ground. Rain angled into the troopship and puddled on the floor panels.

Reaching out to pull the door closed, Gadgets's hand grasped nothing. They had unbolted the doors and left them in the desert outside Culiacan the night before. Gadgets searched through his backpack and pulled out a wallet-sized packet. Unfolding a plastic poncho, he asked Coral, "Ever been to Laos?"

Coral shook his head.

Gadgets looked out at the muddy earth, the sheets of rain, the shadows of the Yaqui sentries, the green forms of the trees fading into the gray sky.

"Helicopters and rain," he said. "Takes me back to those thrilling days of yesteryear, when I was a teenager in Laos."

"Was that a war? How long have you been fighting?"

"Forever. The wars never stop."

Voices and laughter came from the falling rain. Feet splashed through the mud. Three barefoot children ran to the helicopter and looked inside. When they saw Coral and Gadgets, the children dashed away, laughing, pointing imaginary weapons at one another as they ran through the rain.

IN HIS OFFICE AT RANCHO CORTEZ, Lieutenant Colonel Alvarez read the report prepared by Captain Gomez in Culiacan. He studied every detail, noting how the information supported his own suspicions concerning the mysterious battles in the Sierra Madre.

The lieutenant colonel, in the absence of Colonel Gonzalez, now served as acting commandant of the base and the International Group. Though he had assigned patrols to search the mountains for their commanding officer or any surviving members of the unit, he did not expect the patrols to find any living soldiers or officers. And in two days of searching, they had not.

Nor had they found the missing helicopter.

The report from Culiacan contained several significant details.

Evidently a gringo had gone into Culiacan for fuel. He killed several federal agents in a street battle before disappearing into traffic.

An officer in the DEA identified the man as an "antiterrorist specialist" from the United States, one of three "specialists" flown in from San Diego to investigate Los Guerreros Blancos.

The DEA officer stated that the specialists had been shot down in the mountains east of Obregon.

Lieutenant Colonel Alvarez remembered the urgent command to set the trap for the specialists. Soldiers of the International Group had waited in trucks, their SAM-7 missiles ready and aimed, until the DEA jet flew over their position. They shot it down. But the passengers apparently had survived.

Then came the series of ambushes in the Sierra Madre, climaxing with the battles where the International Group lost six helicopters, an airplane and several squads of soldiers.

The soldiers searching the mountains had found the wrecks of five helicopters and the plane. One helicopter remained missing.

Now the gringo specialists from the downed DEA jet had appeared in Culiacan looking for fuel.

No one matching the description of the specialist had been seen at the Culiacan airport. No flights had been spotted at the several dirt airstrips in the area.

Only a helicopter could land without a runway.

Lieutenant Colonel Alvarez began to write down his thoughts. Eventually he went to the communications room and transmitted his notes to Mexico City.

ABLE TEAM AND THE YAQUIS spent the night in a house a hundred meters from the parked helicopter. For five hundred pesos, the family of the orchard's caretaker had chased out the chickens and swept the dirt floor. Rain hammered the corrugated-steel roof all through the afternoon, then fell off to infrequent downpours.

Blancanales and Coral took a bus into Tepic and returned two hours later with boxes of groceries. They had arranged for aviation-quality kerosene to be delivered to the orchard.

"Any trouble?" Gadgets asked them.

Shaking his head, Blancanales passed out beers and dinners. The *carnitas* and tortillas came wrapped in banana leaves. Blocks of ice chilled several six-packs of beer.

In the opposite corner of the one-room house, Lyons interrogated Gunther. Since the capture of the Fascist International officer, Lyons had questioned Gunther at every opportunity, asking endless questions, considering the answers, then rephrasing his questions and asking again. Coral questioned Gunther in Spanish. Working together, Lyons and Coral attempted to trick Gunther into revealing details within the lies of his answers.

Now Lyons was done. He crossed the house to Coral and Blancanales. Coral asked him in a low voice, "What has he told you?"

"Nothing. It's a game. He knows what I'm doing."

"Now I talk with him." Coral went over to Gunther.

The rain pounding on the metal roof covered their voices. As Coral questioned Gunther in Spanish, Lyons briefed Blancanales.

"He's a professional. He probably knows interrogation techniques better than we do."

"What have you said about where we're going?" Blancanales asked. "What have you told him that we'll be doing with him?"

"I told him it depends on how much he helps us."

As Coral rephrased one of Lyons's questions in Spanish, Gunther watched the North Americans. The rain hammering on the roof filled the house with noise. No one heard him when he asked Coral a quick question. "Did you telephone?"

Coral answered quickly. "No. The Puerto Rican was with me every moment. The truck comes tonight. I will try to call tonight."

"He comes." Then Gunther raised his voice. "I know nothing about the operations in Mexico."

Lyons returned with a six-pack of Dos Equis and four dinners. He motioned Coral over to stand guard outside while he rearranged the ropes binding Gunther so that the prisoner could feed himself. The colonel waited until Coral left, then took the opportunity to propose a deal.

"American, I am your prisoner now. But the situation may be reversed in the future. The others cannot hear. Listen to my offer. The International pays better than any government. I get two thousand dollars a week, in gold. You could do very well for yourself."

"I don't fight for money," Lyons said matter-of-factly.

"You risk your life for ideals? Truth, justice and the American Way? But that is government propaganda. You are a professional. You know wars are fought only for money. And your own leaders are with us. Do you think we could move from country to country without their support? Don't be naive. That is for teenagers and charities."

Though Lyons freed Gunther's hands for eating, the prisoner's wrists remained linked by a length of nylon rope. Another length of rope linked the wrist-to-wrist rope to his feet, so that Gunther could not use the short length as a garrote. He was able to eat, but not fight or stand or kick.

The two men sat facing each other, drinking beer and eating tamales and strips of fried beef and chicken rolled into tortillas. The scents of the barbecued meat and cilantro and corn tortillas replaced the musty odors of the adobe house.

Gunther drained a beer in two gulps. "Mexican beer...." He belched. "An advantage of working in Mexico."

"That and the gold, right?"

"You could start at a thousand dollars a week. Are you interested, American?"

Lyons opened another beer for his prisoner. He glanced over his shoulder at his partners, then passed the beer to Gunther.

"I have my ideals."

"We all do. A thousand a week, paid in gold. A starting salary."

"Paid into a numbered account?"

"Automatically. Are you interested?"

Lyons nodded.

5

Twenty miles from the center of Washington, District of Columbia, in an electronics theater at Fort Meade, headquarters of the National Security Agency, two officers studied a computer-enhanced video projection of the topography of the Sierra Madres Occidental. The senior NSA officer, a white-haired man with a face weathered by tropical sun, touched a key on a control panel.

The black-and-white satellite image expanded, the fracture patterns of lines and shapes becoming individual hills and canyons. A black mark broke the mottled grays of one area. When the senior officer touched the keys of the controls again, the image shifted to center on the black spot. Then the image expanded again.

Light reflected from the metal and glass in the wreckage of the Lear jet. The image expanded until the outline of the burned jet filled the screen.

The younger officer spoke. ''Now follow the line of approach back.''

The image shifted to reveal the scar where the crash-landing jet had plowed through the desert brush.

''It landed intact,'' the young officer continued. ''It went in under the pilot's control. After the plane got hit by the rockets, the pilot maintained control long enough to put the plane down. If we had the resolution, we could probably see their footprints going into the brush. I'm willing to bet they torched the plane themselves to confuse the ground forces.''

"Did they get any messages out?"

"There was a Mayday call. They even said, 'We're going down. We are hit by rockets from the Mexican army.' We erased the tapes. No inquiry will ever hear that.''

"Any messages to their superiors?"

"Didn't have the time or the transmission power. And they don't work that way. On their missions, they go in, they make their hit, they come out. Sometimes they hit targets of opportunity. Usually no one knows what they've done until the debriefing. Stony Man is a very special operation. Very loose.''

"Impossible to anticipate.''

"That's it. Punch in those other coordinates.''

The older man touched the keyboard. The screen flashed and another satellite image appeared. On the whorls and lines of this image, they saw a cluster of wrecks. The senior officer touched a key and the image expanded.

They saw a flat hill littered with the wreckage of four helicopters. The senior man shook his head at the sight.

"Millions of dollars of the International's equipment. What exactly did those hotshots carry in with them?"

"Rifles, pistols.''

"They didn't do that with rifles.''

"They seem to be operating with indigenous forces. That's the report from Mexico."

"What indigenous forces?"

"Indians."

"What?"

"That's what Mexico says. Seems Indians are growing opium in the mountains. There have always been gang wars for the control of the production, so the farmers had their own militias, men with shotguns and rifles to protect the crops. Then, when the International sent in the Mexican army to organize the opium farmers, things went crazy. The militias wiped out army patrols and took their weapons. Now the militias have got automatic rifles, machine guns, mortars. Their armament matches the army, because it *is* the army's—"

"Including a helicopter."

"They believe so. The army sent in six helicopter troopships and a light plane. They've only found the wreckage of the plane and five troopships. Now they've got reports of the Able Team hotshots in Culiacan trying to buy fuel."

"What's the range of that model of helicopter?" asked the senior man.

"It could make Culiacan. The locals had agents at the airport and the doper landing strips around the city. Nothing. So I pulled a computer analysis of both areas. Visual spectrum and infrared of the mountains around the fighting and the desert around Culiacan. No helicopter. Not that that means anything, of course. They could have it covered. But it's a spooky situation. They could show up anywhere."

"Why wouldn't they go north to the border?"

"Oh, let's hope they get that stupid. If they fly for the border, they'll come into our radar. Or if they put out a transmission and identify themselves, no matter where they are, we'll zap them so fast they won't know what hit them."

LIEUTENANT SOTO OF THE 5TH ARMY DIVISION of the republic of Mexico turned from Highway 15 and guided his jeep through the ruts and flooded sink-holes of the pueblo's road. The previous day's storm had flooded the fields and washed soil and branches into the road, but the jeep's low gear powered through the mud and debris.

He consulted the map that a local policeman had drawn for him. Passing the row of houses lining the road, he turned down the intersecting road, not actually a road but two deep ruts cutting through the thick grass.

He saw the grove ahead of him. The tires of a heavy truck had flattened the grass. He saw places where the truck had bogged down and spun its tires, digging holes in the ruts and spraying the roadside with mud.

He thought this odd. His map showed another road that trucks utilized to take produce to market. No truck driver would take his vehicle through mud and soggy grass when he could use a gravel road.

Unless the driver had been unfamiliar with the area.

In his duties as an investigative assistant in the division's antidrug and anticontraband office, Lieutenant Soto had driven through all the back roads of the state of Nayarit. And he had encountered all the tricks and mistakes of the smugglers. He had found airstrips planted with corn. He had arrested North American surfers in San Blas as they refueled seaplanes from boats. He had found the wreckage of a plane, stinking with corpses and bloody marijuana, that crashed after torrential rain had doused the fires marking their landing field.

But smugglers using an army of Mexico helicopter?

When he first received the report of the helicopter down in an orchard, he had thought it could only be as told: an army troopship had been caught in the storm and had landed. But when he called the sergeant responsible for the scheduling of helicopter flights, the sergeant told him all the division's helicopters had been grounded by the weather.

Grounded at the division base.

Then he called the federal offices. No helicopters missing. Calls to the army units in the states of Jalisco and Zacateca found no missing helicopters.

Now the lieutenant would see whether the policeman's report had been true in the first place.

Glancing to the penciled map from time to time, he followed the lane, and the truck tracks, to the avocado grove. He saw deep marks in the mud where the truck had cut between the rows of trees. The lieutenant followed the tracks.

He saw the caretaker's house. A few hundred meters farther he came to another house. He stopped the jeep. Stepping through the thick mulch of matted leaves and red mud, he went to the door and knocked. The door swung open.

A dog ran out. The lieutenant looked inside. The single room of the house had been recently swept. Looking down at the concrete step, he saw chicken feathers and the smears of rain-soaked droppings.

Inside, he saw only cardboard boxes of trash. The dog had overturned the boxes to gnaw on chicken bones and stale tortillas. Beer cans had rolled everywhere.

Bootprints marked the floor. He stepped into the dirt. The prints of his army-issue boots matched the prints on the floor.

The lieutenant paced through the interior, looking for any other sign of an army squad—ration cartons, broken equipment, initials carved in the whitewashed walls—but he found nothing. Only the bootprints and the boxes of trash remained of the strangers that the policeman had reported stayed the night here.

He did not return to his jeep. Instead, he followed the bootprints into the grove. He noticed the prints of other boots, different from the army-issue boots. Some of the prints indicated men of normal size, other prints suggested very large men. He attempted to estimate the number of men by counting the bootprints, but the boots crossed and recrossed and obscured one another. He could determine only that there had been several soldiers and two large men.

Following the prints to a clearing in the grove, he saw the cut leaves and branches. He looked at the branches above his head and saw that the branches had been trimmed off in an approximate circle. As if by rotor blades.

The bootprints led to the center of the clearing, where they stopped.

The tire tracks of the truck cut through the mud to the center of the clearing, then stopped too.

Rainwater filled the parallel marks of helicopter skids. He paced the marks and finally confirmed the policeman's report.

A helicopter, of the type used to carry troops, had parked there overnight.

Witnesses had reported the landing of a military helicopter. But the Mexican army and the federals reported no helicopters in service during the storm.

Who had a UH-1 troopship painted with the insignia of the army of Mexico?

Why had they avoided the airport, only twenty kilometers away, to park for the night in an avocado orchard?

And what had they transferred from the truck to the helicopter?

Lieutenant Soto did not know. But he would know soon.

IN A COW PASTURE outside the city of Morelia, Lyons negotiated with Colonel Gunther.

In the chill high-altitude air, the others crowded around the warmth of a small fire. Wind swept down the mountainsides above them, swaying the pines that concealed them. No one had a coat or shelter except Davis, who slept in the pilot's compartment of the Huey.

That afternoon, after they had landed in the concealment of the pines, Blancanales and Coral left to buy aviation kerosene at the Morelia airport, thirty kilometers away. Until they returned with fuel for the helicopter and food for the passengers, Lyons and Gunther could talk without interruption.

"It would be a waste of your potential to actually leave your unit and join us," Gunther told him. "You have proven yourself to them. You are trusted. You could contribute invaluable information to the International. And perhaps without compromising your missions."

"What do you mean?"

"Your superiors do not limit your unit's missions to only actions against the International, correct?"

"Right. We go up against problems as they come along. Sometimes Communist terrorists, sometimes criminals, right-wing groups, whoever."

"You could keep us informed, but we would only communicate with you when your missions threatened our operations. Then we would issue instructions to you."

"Like what?"

"To overlook an individual. To lead the mission to a false conclusion. These things could be arranged so that your unit appears to always succeed. Yet the International's operations would continue untouched. We have similar arrangements with others."

"Who? The FBI, the CIA?"

Gunther nodded. "And the other services. Some work with us directly, others work as you will, others work in complete ignorance of who actually receives the assistance they furnish. It is an excellent system. The divisions and departments maintain security and greatly expand our areas of operation."

"How do I know you won't just have us wiped out sometime? It would be easy. I tell you we have an op coming up, you put out a unit to off us. Or you let the Libyans or the Soviets know and they do it."

"That would not be in our interest."

"But how would I protect myself against that?"

"You have information to use against me," Gunther reminded the American.

"Maybe. All I know is what you told me about your operations in the United States. Nothing to act on. Like you say, you're departmentalized. If it's true."

"What I told you is true. That information bought me time. I had to prove my value to you. I had no other hope of survival."

"And how do I prove myself to your organization?"

"My freedom. And immediate information."

"What information?"

"Why are you going south? You could have flown north to the American border."

"We wouldn't have made it to the border. The Mexicans and the U.S. have downward-looking radar covering the approach to the border. No matter how low we flew, the radar or the satellites would have tracked us. The DEA already arranged to have us shot down once. We can't push our luck."

"But why Mexico City?"

"Coral has friends from the Ochoa gang there."

Hearing that information, Gunther nodded.

"They can arrange for a charter flight north," Lyons continued. "We figured that was the only way to get a prisoner north."

"But once we arrive in Mexico City, that problem is over, correct?"

"If you escape, do you have people who can help you get out of Mexico?"

Gunther nodded.

Lyons looked around, then spoke. "Then that's when I start earning my gold," he said.

LATER IN THE NIGHT, Coral returned. He discussed the questioning of Gunther with Lyons and Blancanales, then he went to question the prisoner himself. But he did not question him about the International.

"What has the blond one said?" Coral asked.

"He said he wants the gold."

"He'll turn against the others?"

"Perhaps it is the truth. But I think he is lying. He will not join the Reich. Not for the victory. Not for the gold. Americans have their ideals."

6

Forested mountainsides stood like a wall against the clouded sky. Davis took the helicopter higher and higher, the turbine whine becoming a shriek, the rotor blades slashing thinner atmosphere with every meter of elevation. The helicopter entered the clouds, mist swirling through the interior, the forest suddenly gone. For a moment, enveloped in the clouds, the noise of the turbine overwhelming their thoughts and senses, they floated in a cold, gray void.

Flashes of daylight came, then the helicopter broke from the clouds. A brilliant blue sky domed the Valley of Mexico. Vato shouted over the turbine noise and pointed to the southeast.

"There." He pointed to the two snow-topped volcanoes. "Popocatepetl. Iztaccihuatl. We are near *la ciudad*."

But a gray pall denied any sight of the world's largest city. In the center of the valley, a point of light flashed as sunlight blazed from the polished metal of an airliner descending into the pollution generated by millions of autos and trucks and factories in the distant Mexican capital.

Lyons spoke into the intercom. "How much farther?"

"We're there," Davis replied.

"But it looks like we're still thirty or forty miles away."

"We are, specialist. But I know Mexico City. Take my word for it, this is as close as we'll get with the Huey. As soon as I spot a road, I'm putting this thing down."

"Make it somewhere isolated," Lyons told him. "We might have to leave it parked for days."

Blancanales spoke through the intercom. "This is it for the helicopter. Miguel and I will go into the city and rent cars."

"We can't abandon this helicopter," Lyons argued. "It could be our ticket out if we fall into a bad situation down there—"

Davis interrupted. "Then you fly it. This thing's done fifteen hundred miles without servicing. Flying it one more minute than we need to is chancing a very sudden descent. I want to park it and walk away."

"This is a million-dollar machine!" Lyons protested.

"Yeah?" Davis retaliated. "Isn't that what I said when you burned the Lear jet? Listen to me. This million-dollar machine is trashed. The joyride is over. Let the Mexicans repossess it. There's our road—no villages, no farms, just canyons and trees. Looks good."

Below them, trees covered steep hillsides. A gravel road followed the curves and folds of a mountainside. They saw a trail along a ridge line. On another ridge line, tire ruts led from the gravel road to a wide clearing. The mature trees had been harvested, then the cleared ground replanted with seedlings among the stumps.

"Miguel!" Gadgets called out. He plugged a second set of headphones into the NSA secure-frequency radio captured from the International Group. Coral slipped on the headphones. He listened as Gadgets plugged in a cassette tape recorder.

"What's going on?" Lyons asked him.

Gadgets motioned for him to wait.

The helicopter banked. Gaining altitude, they flew over the ridge crest. The road disappeared in the trees. They saw flat stone slabs and low brush on a hilltop.

"What do you think of that place, the rocks down there?" Davis asked through the intercom.

"You're driving," Lyons told him.

"One last look," Davis said.

Davis took the helicopter in a quick orbit of the hilltop. Lyons and the Yaquis sat in the door. In the valley beyond, more than three kilometers from the hilltop, they saw the geometry of farms: rectangular fields, the lines of cornstalks, the circles of ponds. Smoke drifted from trees concealing houses. But they saw no fields or trails near the flat hilltop itself.

Seconds later, the skids scraped rock. Dust and leaves swirled around the helicopter. Davis shut down the turbine. Only the rush of the slowing rotors broke the silence. Then the rotors stopped.

Wind carried away the odor of burned kerosene. The Yaquis straightened their uniforms and stepped from the gaping doors. Glancing at Gadgets, Miguel and Blancanales listening to the NSA radio, Lyons followed the Yaquis out.

Birds and insects broke the silence with their sounds. FN FAL paratroop rifles slung over their backs, the Yaquis walked into the forest. Jacom and Kino searched downhill, Ixto uphill. Lyons followed Vato. Staying two steps behind the slight young man, Lyons watched him move silently through the brush, listening for every sound, his head pivoting to scan the trees and lush foliage for any sign of observers.

Tropical trees blocked the sun. Spots of light glowed on ferns and flowering plants. Vato moved effortlessly through the foliage. He stopped. Lyons saw Vato watching something. Then he too saw it.

A hummingbird, resplendent in shimmering emerald-green feathers, hovered only an arm's reach from Vato. When the bird moved, flashing from shadow to sunlight, the young man followed. Vato and Lyons wove through the trees and ferns, around a clump of bayonetlike maguey cactus, and stopped at a sheer wall of rock overhung by trees.

Hummingbirds chattered. Lyons looked around and saw more of the tiny birds, hovering and darting around a flowering tree, their wings blurs, their bodies like jewels floating in the shadows and light.

Vato reached into the tree to pick a round yellow fruit. He passed one to Lyons.

"Zapote."

They sat among the ferns and grasses, eating *zapotes*. Inside a thin skin, a *zapote* has flesh that tastes like mango, but with the consistency and texture of pudding. Vato smashed a *zapote* on the rock beside him. He and Lyons sat still. Hummingbirds flocked to the *zapote* pulp and took the juices through their needle beaks, emerald wings blurring against the gray stone, the brilliant red of their breast feathers vivid against the soft yellow of the *zapote*.

Vato broke the peace of the moment. "You fear death?"

"I would if I thought about it. But I won't get the chance to think when it comes."

"You're not Christian? You don't believe in heaven?"

Lyons shook his head.

"Don't fear death. Look." Vato pointed to the brilliant blur of a hummingbird. "A warrior reborn. That is what the Nahuatls believe. The reward for a life of courage is rebirth as beauty."

Lyons thought of his lover and fellow warrior, Flor Trujillo, reduced to scorched bones and ashes in the desert outside San Diego.

He reached out to one of the birds with a hand that had caressed Flor, and the bird hovered around his hand. The needle beak touched him. A tongue flicked the *zapote* nectar from his fingers.

Flor had been Catholic. She had worn a crucifix and attended mass and gone to confession. Unconsciously, even though he rejected her beliefs, Lyons had thought of Flor's life and death within the tenets of her religion. He hoped that her God had granted her forgiveness and an eternity of peace. But she had made love without being married and had fought and killed—all sins to her church. Vato's Nahuatl mythology comforted Lyons. Instead of thinking of Flor condemned to an eternity of suffering and torment in the Catholic hell, now he would always imagine her reborn as one of these living jewels. Lyons laughed at his sentimentality.

"You laugh at what I tell you?"

"Thanks for telling me it," Lyons said, smiling, "but they're only birds."

DAVIS AND THE YAQUIS carried cut branches to camouflage the helicopter. Sitting in the door, Gadgets and Coral and Blancanales listened to the NSA radio. On the other side of the troopship, separated from the radio by the transmission housing, Gunther still sat in the doorgunner's seat, tied, blindfolded, wads of cloth taped over his ears.

Lyons and Vato had returned from their patrol. Lyons went to Gadgets's side and asked in a whisper, "What do you have on the radio?"

"Voice of the Reich," Gadgets answered, his voice low.

"What's the plan?"

"I'm going into the city," Blancanales told Lyons. "Miguel will go with me. Davis's Spanish is good; he'll stay here with Gadgets to monitor. When we come back, maybe tonight, maybe tomorrow, we'll have cars. And clothes for Vato and the others. Then we'll do the DF number on the colonel."

"Vato's just told me he wants to try a chemical interrogation first," Lyons reported.

Blancanales looked to the Yaqui leader. "Chemical?" he asked him. "You mean drugs?"

Vato nodded. "Ancient drugs. There will be no marks on his body, but he will reveal everything."

"How long will it take? And what are the aftereffects?"

"A day. And maybe he will be confused and dizzy for another day. Like taking pills."

"It could help us," Lyons said, lowering his voice to a whisper. "We get what info we can, then let him escape. If he's disoriented, he's more likely to make a mistake and go straight to the International."

"What?" Vato asked. "Why will—"

"The plan is to release him. We'll put direction finders on him, then when he runs, we'll follow him."

"Electronic devices? What if he finds them? What if there is interference from the electricity and the radios and the buildings in the city?"

"That's a risk. But I think it will work."

"He'll expect a trick and take precautions."

"Best we can do, under the circumstances."

"No!" Vato protested. "You will not!"

Blancanales intervened. "So we'll try your drug interrogation first. There will be no torture? No physical damage?"

"When I joined my people," Vato told them, "the *achai* gave it to me. To learn about me. There is no harm."

Voices came from the NSA radio. Gadgets turned to Lyons and said, "Get Gunther out of here! He could hear this."

Coral motioned Lyons to stay put. "I will take him away," he said.

Leaving the others, Coral went around the helicopter. He untied the ropes securing Gunther to the doorgunner's seat. Then he untied one of the ropes binding the prisoner's ankles. Gunther required help to step down to the rocks. A second rope around Gunther's ankles served to hobble him.

Able Team took no chances with the six-foot-five,

two-hundred-twenty-pound Gunther. When they had seen the karate-caused calluses on the striking edges of the fascist colonel's hands, they had known they could never allow Gunther to free an arm or leg.

Leading the blindfolded prisoner to the far side of the clearing, Coral tied him to a tree. Then he removed the wads of cloth covering Gunther's ears.

"We are near Mexico City."

"Where?"

"In the mountains. Southwest of the city. There is a problem. It is something I cannot stop."

"What?"

"They will interrogate you with drugs. They are talking about it now."

"The blond one suggested this?"

"No, one of the Yaquis."

"What does the blond one say?"

"He says he will release you and then follow you to your organization."

"He does want the gold! He did exactly what I suggested. This is very good for the International—"

"Forget the International!" Coral interrupted Gunther. "This endangers everything. When you talk, I go to prison. And there will be no escape for my family. My wife and children are with the Drug Enforcement Agency in the United States."

"We have friends in the American agency. They can arrange for the release of your family."

"But what of my freedom? My life? If you say anything under the drugs, I'm dead. Or in prison. We must escape now."

"Do you have a rifle?"

"No."

"Where are the others?"

"The North Americans are in the helicopter. The Yaquis stand guard."

"Then it is not possible now. We will wait."

"But we must escape now!"

"Do not panic, my friend. There is nothing to fear. Drugs will not break me. We will wait until a better time."

"Are you sure? Absolutely sure?"

Still blindfolded, Gunther turned to Coral's voice. "What is the problem? Listen to me. They trust you. When they question me with the drug, they will crowd around me. You will prepare to strike. Be near a weapon. If, under the influence of the drug, I speak, then you kill them. Except for the American who works for us."

7

Lines of taillights disappeared into the gray night of Mexico City. In two rented Mitsubishi minivans, Able Team and the others waited for the traffic to move. The headlights of cars and trucks leaving the city streaked past them. But their lanes remained jammed.

Around them, horns sounded in one unending chord of noise. Passengers leaned from bus windows to look ahead. Truck drivers gestured and cursed. Only motorcycles continued moving, the macho young men—without helmets—accelerating, braking, weaving between the cars and trucks and buses, then accelerating again.

On both sides of the Viaducto, an eight-lane expressway, four lanes in each direction, the nightlife of the Mexican capital buzzed. Without a glance to the traffic only steps away, men clustered under the neon lights of a bar. Boys kicked a soccer ball along the sidewalk. Indian women in satin blouses and cotton skirts sold candy and cigarettes and comic books from curbside stands. Teenagers strolled arm-in-arm through the crowds.

The pastel colors of the shopfronts, vivid pinks and blues and yellows, glowed like the neon of the shops' signs. But other than the painted colors of the shops and cars and the clothing of the people, the North Americans saw only the grays and black of concrete and asphalt. No trees or flowers or lawns lined the streets.

Pollution had killed all but human life. Exhaust from the stalled traffic swept the adjoining streets like fog. A block from the Viaducto, the pollution paled the lights. A few kilometers away, where the skyscrapers of the city towered above the avenues of the business district, the smog grayed the thousands of office lights to abstract smears.

And above the city, the smoke from the thousands of factories and millions of vehicles made a gray dome of pollutants that blocked any sight of the stars or moon.

In the vans, Able Team waited for the traffic to move. Blancanales and Coral had rented the minivans from a tourist agency earlier in the day. Then they drove through the vast city, stopping at shops to buy clothes for the Yaquis, black plastic tarps to cover the helicopter and luggage to conceal the arsenal of captured weapons. Now, in the backs of the vans, overnight bags held pistols and Uzis, suitcases concealed folding-stock rifles and an M-79 grenade launcher, and shipping trunks contained M-60 machine guns. Other trunks carried the NSA securefrequency radios captured from the Mexican army. The suitcases and trunks filled the backs of the vans to the roof.

As Coral idled the engine of the van, waiting for the traffic jam to break up, Lyons sat in the back seat with his feet on Colonel Gunther. Tied and blindfolded, wrapped in a tarp, the prisoner lay on the floor. Vato sat beside Lyons. The Yaqui leader kept his right hand in an airline flight bag. The bag concealed the sawed-off Remington 870 shotgun taken from a dead gunman in Culiacan.

Lyons concealed his Atchisson, fitted with the fourteen-inch "urban-environment barrel," under a clutter of tourist maps on the seat.

If Gunther attempted to escape, Lyons or Vato would execute him. They could not allow him to rejoin the International.

The forces of the Fascist International searched for them. Throughout the afternoon and evening, Gadgets had monitored transmissions between International units. Snatches of conversation—from a private airport, from trucks on the highway—indicated that the commander of the International had withdrawn squads from Culiacan and Rancho Cortez and repositioned the soldiers along the Mexico-United States border. Other units maintained surveillance of Mexico City's airport, watching for North Americans matching the descriptions of the three men of Able Team.

But Able Team hoped to find, and hit, the International first.

The traffic moved. As Coral shifted gears and accelerated, Lyons spoke into his hand-radio. The earphone he wore eliminated any chance of Gunther's overhearing the conversation.

"Wizard, what have you got?"

"Same noise from the boys."

"Like what?"

"A goon said he's leaving. I don't know who, I don't know where, but he's going by air."

"Any addresses?"

Gadgets cut his jive. "Ironman, these Nazis are professionals. Even with the encoding radios, they maintain very tight-mouthed discipline. They're using code names and numbers for their positions. And there's another encrypting radio out there putting out screech transmissions. Not only are they professionals, not only do they have all the modern electronics, but also they seem to be one step ahead of us. I get the scary feeling they could be decoding *us* right now."

"Not possible." Lyons knew that without one of the three secure-frequency radios Able Team carried, no one could monitor their communications.

"Positive?"

"I hope it's not possible."

"Yeah, let's hope. Problem is, the same people who made the radios for us good guys made the radios for those bad guys."

"We don't know that."

"Hey, man, maybe you don't know it. But I know it."

They passed a stadium. Thousands of Mexicans crowded from the ultramodern structure of curved concrete and steel. Traffic slowed again as the cars of the sports fans sped onto the Viaducto. A city policeman directed traffic around an accident.

The wheels of the Mitsubishi crunched over smashed soda-pop cans. To the side of the wide expressway, the driver of a truck argued with a bleeding man who leaned against a smashed Volkswagen. The truck driver pointed to his spilled load of soda-pop cases, then shouted into the face of the injured man.

"The joys of the big city," Lyons commented to Vato.

Vato nodded. He leaned forward and spoke in Spanish to Coral. Then Vato turned to Lyons. "We will be there soon."

Coral had called associates from the Ochoa Gang and negotiated for the use of an auto-repair garage in the slums of Colonia Netzahualcoyotl. He had told them he needed a place to park two vans of contraband "from the north," videotape recorders and videocassettes of American and European pornography. The auto garage would allow the group to arrive and depart without being seen on the street.

Riding through the city, Lyons watched the unending urban sprawl float past. He began to doubt the wisdom of searching the Mexican capital for the headquarters of the International.

On maps, Mexico City looked like yet another of the world's largest cosmopolitan cities.

Back in the isolation of the Sierra Madre of Sonora, Lyons had thought they could search the city. After all, his partners spoke Spanish. They had Mexican allies. They had taken a fascist colonel prisoner. And Lyons himself had lived most of his life in the second largest Mexican city: Los Angeles, California.

As a detective with the Los Angeles Police Department, Lyons had operated in Mexican communities. He had searched for felons in the barrios of Los Angeles and he'd found the criminals. He expected to do the same in Mexico City.

But the street map of the city, mere lines and colors printed on paper, did not communicate the unimaginable scale of the capital of Mexico. Tourist guide-books gave the population as fourteen million. Unof-ficially, the Mexican government estimated that at least eighteen million people lived in the metropolitan center and the satellite cities. In fact, the Mexican government did not know how many millions lived in the vast city.

But going there had avoided an assault on the stronghold of the International's forces in northwest Mexico. Los Guerreros Blancos and the corrupt In-ternational Group of the Mexican Army maintained an army with modern weapons and communications at Rancho Cortez.

An attack on a military base with a force of teen-agers and out-of-work gangsters would have risked pointless death.

In contrast, a surprise attack on the Mexico City offices of the American Reich seemed cunning yet obvious.

Cut off the head. . . .

But first they must find the snake.

Lyons heard his hand-radio click. Gadgets's voice came through the earphone. "Ask Coral what the name of this freeway is."

He leaned forward and whispered. "What freeway are we on?"

"Tlalpan. It is a name from the Aztecs."

"Say it again."

Coral pronounced the unfamiliar word for the North American. "Tlal-pan. Say Te-lal in one sound. Tlal. Tlal-pan."

Lyons stuttered the Nahuatl word into his hand-radio. "Te-lal-pan. Tlalpan."

"Oh, shit!" Gadgets cursed.

"What?"

"Ixnay da jive. Da goonies know!"

It took a moment for Lyons to comprehend the nonsense Gadgets talked. And why. He questioned Gadgets to confirm the message. "Are you positive?"

No answer came. Then a voice shouted from the next traffic lane. Lyons saw Gadgets waving from the other Mitsubishi. He slid back his window.

"Lock and load!" Gadgets shouted. "They know we're on Tlalpan. I just heard it. I don't know how, but they must be monitoring us or tracking us or they got us under surveillance. Use your radio only as a last resort and talk jive, understand?"

Lyons shouted back. "We'll run patterns through traffic. If they're behind us, we'll spot them."

"Got it!"

Driven by Blancanales, the other minivan accelerated ahead. Lyons leaned forward to Coral. "Let him get a few hundred yards ahead. Then we'll speed past him. We're trying to spot any cars following us."

Coral nodded. He waited for the space in the next lane, then whipped the van to the right. He continued over one more lane and swerved in front of a truck.

Traffic sped past. Cars rode the bumpers of trucks. Buses accelerated and braked and swerved through rows of trucks. Motorcycles wove everywhere. In the chaos of headlights, Lyons could not identify any surveillance units. He motioned for Coral to accelerate.

Lyons scanned the vehicles in the other lanes, watching for any car or truck changing lanes or racing to follow them. But he saw only the motorized chaos of thousands of Volkswagens, Fiats, Mexican-manufactured Fords competing for position.

Then he saw a Dodge sedan easing from one lane to another, accelerating smoothly to merge with the flow.

"Miguel, slow down." Lyons turned to Vato. "Take a look at the men in the Dodge. On our left."

In contrast to the dented and dirty compact cars jamming the Viaducto, the powerful Dodge had perfect fenders and a gleaming dark blue finish. As the Dodge passed, Lyons glanced at the shoulders and backs of the passengers. He noted the passengers wore business suits.

A newspaper covered the hands of the man in the front passenger seat. In the back seat, another man held a briefcase, his thumbs on the latches. Then the Dodge passed.

"Two of them are not Mexicans," Vato said.

"And why would executives be going to work at night?" Lyons leaned forward to Coral. "That blue Dodge. Stay near it."

Coral glanced to the rearview mirror. "Behind us. There is another car like that. A white one."

"Tell me when they come up."

Lyons turned to Jacom, who rode in the front passenger seat. He held an Uzi wrapped in a jacket.

As Vato's spotter in the mountain fighting, Jacom had fought the forces of Los Guerreros Blancos and the Mexican army. He had used binoculars to correct Vato's five-hundred-meter rifle fire across the desert wastelands. In the battle at the Hills of the Dead, he had shot down a helicopter troopship with accurate 7.62 NATO slugs into the engine. Now the teenager faced danger in the chaotic traffic of a metropolitan expressway.

Lyons trusted the Yaquis with his life. More than compatriots in arms, Vato and Kino and Ixto and Jacom had become his friends.

A week earlier, Lyons did not know that the teenagers or their mountain people existed. If the cynical ex-LAPD detective had encountered the Yaquis—a tribal militia protecting the opium fields of the Sierra Madre—Lyons would have killed them. But the past week had given Lyons a quick education in the poverty and oppression of Mexico. He knew they grew opium for the heroin factories of Culiacan. He did not excuse their crimes, but now he understood their desperation. Now he would work to turn the people away from the drug trade.

"Ready?" Lyons asked.

Jacom nodded.

As Lyons reached into a suitcase for his Atchisson, he heard tires scream on asphalt.

Metal smashed metal.

Autoweapons fired.

8

Gadgets flicked down the fire-selector of his silenced Beretta 93-R and fired a 3-shot burst into the gunman's face when he saw the Uzi come out from under the newspapers.

The gunman fell sideways across the front seat of the dark blue Dodge. The Dodge swerved into a bus. The drivers of other cars hit their brakes. Bumpers smashed.

The Dodge straightened, and the engine roared as the driver closed the car lengths to the Mitsubishi van. A weapon flashed. Slugs shattered the side windows behind Gadgets and exited through the roof. Gadgets put the tritium night sights of the Beretta on line with the gunman firing from the back seat of the Dodge.

But the driver anticipated the return fire. Tires screaming, the International driver swerved. The Beretta's low-velocity 9mm slugs only cracked the windshield, ricocheting into the night as the Dodge wove behind the minivan, crossing three lanes in an instant.

A truck crashed into the curb fence to avoid the Dodge as another gunman fired an Uzi from the car's left rear window. Davis popped off rounds from a Colt Government Model as high-velocity 9mm slugs hammered the van. The suitcases and trunks behind Gadgets jumped with impact as bullets passed through the thin sheet metal of the Japanese-built compact van. One slug scored a window. Granules of glass showered the interior.

Ixto aimed an autopistol but the Dodge had already swerved away, slipping through the trucks and cars like a shark moving through fish.

"That man can drive!" Gadgets yelled. He watched the Dodge maneuvering for another attack. A dump truck painted with day-glo designs blocked the International's driver from accelerating. Blancanales calmly moved through the traffic, swerving to keep other vehicles between their van and the pursuing gunmen. Gadgets took the reprieve to upgrade his firepower.

Reaching into his backpack, he tore open a plastic case and grabbed two Italian MU-50G controlled-effect grenades. The tiny grenades, designed for the close-quarter combat of antiterrorist actions, had a forty-six-gram charge of TNT to propel 1,400 steel balls. The reduced charge of explosive limited the one hundred percent kill diameter to ten meters.

"Grenades?" Davis asked. "Man, there are innocent people everywhere!"

"It's cool. These are Italian designer grenades. So chic, so cool for a freeway firefight." Gadgets waited for the next attack.

Looking in the rearview mirror, Blancanales shouted, "Here comes another one!"

The second Dodge, the white one, gained on them. Differing from the first Dodge only in color, the second pursuit car also contained four gunmen with submachine guns.

Then they heard the boom of a shotgun. Gadgets grinned to the others. "Ironman to the rescue!"

Lyons leaned from the window of the van that Coral drove and fired into the oversize double rear tires of a freight truck. Tires exploding and flapping on the rim, the heavy truck lurched, the remaining tires smoking as the driver fought for control. The truck slowed, blocking lanes, acting as a traffic barricade.

Coral floored the accelerator. The other cars on the Viaducto pulled to the side to escape the danger of the wild shoot-out.

As Coral gained on the two sedans, Vato shoved aside luggage and crawled into the back of the van. He tried to lift the lid of a shipping trunk. The lid raised only a few inches before being stopped by the roof of the van. By touch, he searched through the interior, finally dragging out an FN FAL para-rifle and a bandolier of box mags. Vato shoved the trunk aside to block the side window. He arranged the suitcases to block the other side windows. Twisting into the narrow space between the shipping trunk and the stacked suitcases, he shoved the FN FAL's barrel through the tempered glass of the back lift-door. He swung out the rifle's metal stock and waited.

Ahead, the two Dodges maneuvered for position, accelerating to make a cross-fire kill on the van that Blancanales drove.

A hand reached out from the van. A tiny ball hit the asphalt, bounced high over the roof of the white Dodge and flashed.

Hundreds of tiny steel balls hit the hood and the windshield and the roof of the Dodge.

But without effect. The steel shrapnel pocked the paint and shattered the windshield but it did not touch the gunmen inside. The driver braked and swerved away.

Gadgets looked back and saw the gunman in the front seat methodically smashing out the laminated safety glass with the steel butt of his Uzi. Another burst of 9mm slugs hit the van as the other Dodge continued the pursuit. Gadgets pulled the pin on a second MU-50G grenade and tossed it, hoping for a hit on the engine or tires.

The tiny grenade bounced over the Dodge, then bounced again on the pavement. The grenade popped twenty meters behind the Dodge, spraying steel through empty air. The Dodge accelerated.

"Italian shit!"

The Atchisson boomed. Gadgets and Davis saw flame streaking from the short barrel of the assault shotgun. Glass exploded from the white Dodge as Lyons swept the back windshield and side windows with semiauto blasts of number-two and double-ought steel shot. Blood splashed the shattered windshield.

Lyons continued firing as Coral accelerated past the white Dodge. Glass and gore sprayed from the far windows, the driver dying, the Dodge skidding sideways. The heavy car smashed into the center divider and overturned, throwing a man from a window. The rolling car smeared him into the asphalt.

"One down!" Gadgets waved as Coral sped past in the other tourist van. He saw Lyons reloading his Atchisson. Looking back, Gadgets aimed his silenced, underpowered Beretta at the pocked windshield of the remaining pursuit car. He semi-autoed round after round at the swerving blue sedan.

A rifle fired from the back of the other Mitsubishi. The 7.62mm NATO slugs tore through the surviving Dodge, punching through steel and flesh. The Dodge slowed as the wounded driver struggled for control. The heavy-caliber battle rifle fired three more times. The big sedan drifted across the lanes, carrying dead and wounded men to a slow, screeching stop against the curb.

In the second van, Coral turned to Lyons. "We must make our vehicles look okay. Soon police will look for us. Tell the others."

Vato had already put away the FN FAL para-rifle. As the minivan sped over the now-deserted freeway, he used his boot to clean the remnants of the shattered glass from the lift-door's window. Lyons leaned out his window and shouted to Blancanales and Gadgets.

"Clean it up! We still got a way to go."

"Doing it already!" Gadgets shouted back. "But what about the bullet holes?"

"No way, no time!"

The Mitsubishi tourist vans entered the traffic of an interchange and left the Viaducto Tlalpan behind. Lyons watched the passengers in the vehicles around him on the expressway. Many of the other people rode with their windows open to the pollution of the warm night. And in the shifting lights and smoke of traffic, no one seemed to notice the 9mm holes in the sheet metal of the minivan.

But the bullet holes would not escape the notice of a policeman.

Coral turned on the dash radio and spun through the stations. He stopped at a news station and listened to the announcer's monologue. "Nothing said yet."

"How much farther?" Lyons asked.

"Very near."

Gunther shifted on the floor. Lyons pressed his shoes down on the fascist colonel's back. As they sped through the evening traffic, Lyons counted the charges they faced if the Mexican authorities arrested them.

Kidnapping. Murder. Assault. Mayhem. Conspiracy. Illegal weapons. Theft of army weapons and equipment. Illegal entry into the country. Currency violations. Speeding. Public nuisance.

If they went to trial, they faced a lifetime in prison. But they would never get to trial. The Fascist International controlled units of the Mexican army and the *Federales*. If the fascists had also infiltrated the metropolitan police, the North Americans would not live long in jail.

But Able Team and the Yaquis had lived through the pursuit and firefight on the Viaducto. Maybe their luck would hold.

Coral left the Viaducto, Blancanales following a moment later in the other minivan. They inched through a jammed intersection, horns and voices loud around them, then Coral turned onto a side street.

Narrow as an alley, with rusting cars and trucks parked on either sidewalks, the street led through a neighborhood of decaying tenements. The smog had long ago stained the concrete and stone of the buildings the same gray black of the starless, moonless night.

Corner streetlights created patterns of brilliance in the gray streets, light reflecting from gutter water and windows and car chrome. But elsewhere on the streets, only lights from windows and doors broke the darkness.

Neon words identified some doorways as businesses. In others, fluorescent tubes cast gray light on racks of broken mailboxes. Shadowy corridors led into darkness.

The windows of some apartments opened directly to the sidewalks. Inside, people occupied rooms bright with plastic furniture. One apartment had posters of Julio Iglesias and the blond singers of Abba. Another showed posters of the Rolling Stones and a defiant Che Guevara.

Above the tenements, an electric billboard advertised Cerveza Tecate with thousands of colored lights, patterns of different colors forming the shape of a beer bottle and spelling out the name.

Finally Coral stopped at a steel rollaway door. Sooty paint above the entry read *Automecánica*. Coral got out of the car and opened a padlock on the door.

Lyons's hand almost keyed his hand-radio. He stopped himself. Instead, he spoke to Vato and Jacom.

"Check the area and look for surveillance. Look for anything unusual. I would do it but—"

Vato understood. "You are too unusual here."

The two young men stepped into the gray night. Vato carried the flight bag concealing the sawed-off Remington 870.

Looking back, Lyons saw Blancanales signal him. Blancanales pointed to the roof lines. Lyons nodded and held up one hand. He cocked back his thumb like a pistol hammer. Then he put his hand back on the pistol-grip of his Atchisson.

Coral returned to the van and drove it inside the garage. Lyons saw two Japanese compact cars parked inside the cavernous garage.

"What are those cars doing there?" he asked.

"We rented four cars," Coral explained. "Rosario wanted backup cars. In case."

"Good. We need them." Lyons stepped into the darkness of the garage, the Atchisson cocked and locked, his thumb on the fire selector.

The darkness smelled of old oil and rot. As Blancanales drove in the other van, Lyons snap-scanned the interior of the garage in the moment of headlights. He saw only walls, bricked-up windows, doorways. He waited until Blancanales switched off the engine. Then he trotted blind through the darkness, stopping short of the doorway.

Behind him, the doors of the minivan opened, the dome light casting a weak glow. Lyons continued slowly to the doorway. Pressing his back to the cold concrete, he listened, the Atchisson gripped at portarms.

He heard movement. A can clanked. Lyons flicked his Atchisson's fire-selector off safety.

The Yaquis came through the entry. Coral pulled down the rolling steel door.

Lyons stood in the semidarkness, still listening for movement. His partners and the Yaquis waved flashlights over the interior, lighting the corners, searching the back of the garage. Shoes clanged on steel as someone ran upstairs, the noise echoing in the empty building.

"*¡Ratones!*" A voice called out.

Lyons heard feet stomping. Squeaking things scurried across the floor, claws scratching.

Lights flashed on, bare bulbs lighting the garage with searing glare. Lyons snapped a glance through a doorway of a small room behind him.

He saw only the mottled gray and brown of rats running for safety.

Taking a breath, Lyons stepped into the room, the Atchisson ready. The room had been the garage office. The window had been bricked shut except for an air slot at the top. Looking up through the slot, he saw the flashing colors of the electric Tecate billboard. Padlocks and chains secured a door to the street. Black dust lined the shelves and stained the walls. On the floor, he saw that shoes had recently crossed the soot-covered linoleum. But he found only rats.

"Ironman!" Gadgets called out. "Where are you and that righteous thundergun going?"

Flicking on the safety of the assault shotgun, Lyons returned to his partners. "This would have been the absolutely perfect ambush. Wait till we close the doors, then bang-bang." Lyons pointed to the backup compact cars. "Have you checked those for booby traps or DF units?"

"Did it first thing."

"Anything on the Nazi radios?"

"I have totally discontinued my monitoring of the electromagnetic spectrum until I check out that NSA radio," Gadgets declared. "Something gave us away. In fact, those gooners zoomed right in on us. I'm going to take that black box radio apart."

"Couldn't have been our radios?"

"Dig it—we had hand-radios in both vans. And we didn't say where we were, nothing like 'Cruising north on Tlalpan Avenue.' "

"Surveillance?" Lyons asked. "Maybe they spotted us coming into the city?"

"In all those thousands of cars?" Gadgets asked, incredulous. "Anyway, don't we have almost identical vans? With Anglos in both vans? You notice they didn't lock on to you.... Man, that means something."

"Yeah. It means they know we're in the city."

"And," Blancanales added, "that we have lost the element of surprise. We may be hunting them, but now they're hunting us, too."

In a van, Coral listened to the dash radio. An announcer raved nonstop. Coral turned to the North Americans.

"It is on the news. On all the stations. They tell of North Americans killing Mexicans and Europeans. This one—" he motioned to the voice blaring from the radio "—a politician says it is CIA. He will demand the withdrawal of United States forces. He is screaming 'Foreign invaders, foreign invaders. *¡Invasión de extranjeros!* ' "

9

History chronicles many invasions of Mexico. The armies of the United States, the French empire, the Catholic empire, all played their role in creating the passionate nationalism of the Mexican people.

Yet the armies of the North American and European nations appear late in the history of the region that would become the republic of Mexico.

In the ancient Valley of Mexico, the black, alluvial soil of the shores of Lake Texcoco provided the foundation of life for the emerging civilization of the Mexicans. The people farmed crops of corn and beans and squash, and the gentle climate and seasons allowed for two crops a year. They lived in union with the seasons of their crops, fearing drought and disease, hoping for ample harvests and many children.

Religion rose from the mystical bonds between these people and their world. Before the Romans built their public monuments on the Mediterranean, pyramids and temples overlooked the mists swirling about Lake Texcoco.

But an accident of geology had formed the valley—with its temperate climate, its fertile land and year-round streams—in the center of regions ravaged by tropical extremes. To the north, barren deserts offered only cactus and small animals to sustain the tribes of nomads living in wastelands. To the south, despite the torrential rains and lush tropical growth, the red clay soil would not support agriculture.

When strangers came to the valley, they saw the paradise of Mexico and wanted it. The mountains circling the valley did not protect the people from the invasions. The ancient people of Mexico knew only unending war.

Cycles of invasion created endless defeat and chaos. A barbarian tribe called the Toltecs entered the Valley of Mexico and attacked the city-states lining the shores of Lake Texcoco. The Toltecs crushed some cities and became allies with others. The religions and traditions merged, the decadent and barbarian cultures fusing. This new culture spoke Nahuatl, the language still spoken in Central Mexico a thousand years later.

The god of war became a vital part of the Nahuatl culture. When Nahuatl-speaking cities built temples, their two supreme gods received the highest and most splendorous pyramids. The first, Quetzalcoatl, the god of the Teotihuacanis, represented enlightenment and beauty. The other, Tezcatlipoca, became the god of war and magic. The gentle priests of Quetzalcoatl— the Plumed Serpent—asked the people only for offerings of jewels and feathers and sacred butterflies. The warrior-priests of Tezcatlipoca—The Smoking Mirror, the Lord of Night—demanded the hearts of captives taken in battle.

Legends tell of Quetzalcoatl inventing the calendar and astronomy and mathematics. Other legends describe the beauty of the god's own city, Tula, where the feather-pennants of his palace floated like shimmering flames. Though archaeology disproves the enrapturing myths of Quetzalcoatl, the reign of the god-king represented the ultimate achievement of Mexican culture.

But Quetzalcoatl fell.

The violent devotees of death, demanding war, demanding human blood and hearts to gorge Tezcatlipoca, overwhelmed Quetzalcoatl.

In time, myth transformed the god-king from a gold-skinned Nahuatl to a being with white skin and a beard, clothed in shimmering metal, who marked his path with crosses. The Toltecs believed Quetzalcoatl would someday return from his exile to retake his throne.

This myth doomed Mexico to conquest by European invaders.

In the centuries following the expulsion of Quetzalcoatl, the Toltecs, who had invaded Mexico, suffered the invasion of the Chichimecs. These tribes of merciless barbarians worshipped a god who spoke only to priests and warriors, Huitzilopochtli. Led by their god, they wandered the valley, attacking the weak cities, making alliances with the strong. Later, one tribe of the Chichimecs established their city on a marshy island in the center of Lake Texcoco. They were the Aztecs.

The Aztecs dedicated their city of Tenochtitlan to war. As their first act, they erected a temple to their god Huitzilopochtli and gave him a sacrifice of the "sacred eagle cactus fruit," human hearts.

Huitzilopochtli demanded unending blood. The Aztec lords believed that if they failed to appease their god's hunger for victims, the sun would fail to rise. They sacrificed their own young men and the warriors of other nations. The Aztecs fought their wars not to expand their empire, but to take captives for the altar of their god. Ceremonies demanded hearts. At the dedication of a new pyramid to Huitzilopochtli, the Aztecs sacrificed eighty thousand captured warriors in four days.

Sacrifice decimated the young men of the defeated nations. Taxes impoverished the citizens. But invincible armies of Aztec warriors threatened any rebellious nation of their empire with annihilation.

Then couriers brought word of the return of Quetzalcoatl. The couriers told of floating mountains coming from the east, bringing a man with white skin and a beard, clothed in metal. The white man brought an army of superhuman white warriors who walked on four legs, preceded by priests with crosses.

And so the Spanish marched into Mexico. Every enemy of the Aztecs believed that alliance with the Spanish offered release from centuries of domination by the Aztec warrior-priests. With the gunpowder weapons and the horses of the European invaders, they hoped to smash the armies of the Aztec empire and win freedom for their people.

Together, the Spanish and their Mexican allies destroyed the Aztecs.

But instead of granting their allies freedom, the Europeans ravaged the Mexican nations and cultures in a holocaust unequaled in Mexican history for savagery and murder. The Spanish conquerors of Mexico claimed the wealth of the conquered land as theirs by the divine right of victory. The looting of the gold of Tenochtitlan, the enslavement of the defeated warriors, the mass rapes of the starving widows and daughters of the defeated, the destruction of the temples for building stone...Spanish greed and lust had no limit: not law, not conscience, not human pity. What the Spanish saw, they took.

Spanish knives pried out precious stones. Spanish wrecking bars tore the gold and jade and turquoise from the holy places. What had been sacred, beyond price, became only loot.

Cortez took his share and distributed a share to his white warriors. Shares went to the imperial court of Castille to buy perfumes to scent the stinking, never-washed bodies of the nobility, to buy spices for the palace dinners, to buy silks and velvets for the splendor of the royal audience. But the greatest share of the loot went to the king and queen of Spain themselves.

Though the Mexicans continued to fight the Europeans, they suffered defeat after defeat at the steel blades and muskets and cannons of the invaders. If the Mexican warriors avoided the swords and the bullets of the Castillians, smallpox—the most lethal of the Spanish weapons, the weapon that decimated entire cities—eliminated the last organized resistance in central Mexico.

From La Ciudad de Mexico, the Spanish overlords dispatched hundreds of expeditions, numbering from a few soldiers to thousands, to search for other cities with wealth to loot.

To the south and west, they found more lands and peoples to conquer and rape and enslave.

But to the north, the Spanish found desert lands and peoples they could not conquer: the Yaquis, the Comanches, the Apaches.

The Spanish turned to the slavery and exploitation of Mexicans to sustain their wealth. In the mountains where the Spanish found gold or silver, Mexicans broke the stone and carried the ore from the mines. Mexicans slaved day after day, endlessly, without any hope of release but death. The Spanish overlords watched the carrion birds feeding on the emaciated bodies of Mexicans who had been Knights of the Eagle and Jaguar before the destruction of Tenochtitlan, and they called it "God's justice."

Where the Spanish found no precious metals, only fertile land, the conquerors created haciendas. Mexican slaves worked the vast estates. They had no rights, no future but slavery, no hope. They suffered through a life lower than animals, because the animals knew only pain and death, while the Mexicans remembered Mexico before the Spanish and despaired.

Finally, after years of debate between the Spanish and the Catholic Pope, the Church ruled that *los indígenas* had human souls and could receive the Mercy of Christ. The Mexicans received the religion of the Spanish, but the suffering continued.

Spanish colonists flooded Mexico. Year after year, the Spanish overlords exacted wealth without measure from Mexico. The king and queen of Spain appointed viceroys to rule "New Spain." Generations passed as kings and queens of Spain ruled through their viceroys.

By the terms of the First Audiencia, no Spaniard

born in Mexico could hold imperial office. The Spanish born in Mexico, called the Creoles, resented this dictatorial ban. Pure Castillian blood flowed through their veins, they spoke the language of the court, they attended universities in Europe, and yet they did not enjoy the opportunity for prestige and enrichment offered by the Imperial Office of Viceroy.

Centuries passed without change. Then, in Spain, King Ferdinand VII lost his throne to Joseph Bonaparte of France. The Creoles, who had tolerated the rule and taxation of a Spanish emperor for generations, refused to share the wealth of Mexico with a French emperor. The Creoles demanded independence for New Spain.

Mexicans also demanded independence. In a decade of civil turmoil, an alliance of the Creole elite—the Church, the army, and the landowning "families"—defeated armies of *indígenas* and mestizos—Mexicans of mixed European and Indian blood—who wanted national independence, freedom from slavery and the distribution of land to the people. Mexico gained independence from Spain, but now the Spanish Creoles ruled the Mexicans.

One hundred years of violence and dictatorship passed before the Revolution. But the traditions of slavery and feudal domination did not end. The Creole elite never forgot their Spanish birthright of wealth and privilege.

Though the blond hair and fair skin of the Spanish had been darkened through the generations, the Creole elite continued to rule from Mexico City. They spoke Castillian. They honored the European conceits of racial superiority. They sent their children to European universities. They never surrendered their control of the government.

This aristocracy of modern Mexicans who traced their ancestry to Castille continued the tradition of the exploitation of Mexico. Their Spanish forefathers stole the gold of Tenochtitlan. The Creoles stole the land and enslaved the Mexicans. The modern elite exploited the "liberated" campesinos and workers. The elite found foreign co-conspirators—North Americans and Europeans—to rob Mexico of natural resources. The elite made illegal contracts for the delivery of minerals, wood and oil, then invested their foreign earnings in Swiss banks and political bribes.

Indígenas and mestizos sometimes held the presidency of Mexico, but the elite always held the government. Campesinos received plots of land, but the elite held vast, fertile valleys, watered by rivers, financed by its own banks. *Indígenas* found work in industry, but the elite owned the factories. Some villages received water and electricity, but the elite enjoyed Cancun and Paris. Mexicans voted, but the elite selected the candidates.

Then, in 1970, the intensely nationalist administration of President Luis Escheverria threatened the control exerted by the wealthy. Land reforms cut into the vast holdings of the leading Creole "families." Taxes took a share of their profits to provide schools and hospitals for the people of Mexico. The emergence of a distinctly Mexican culture, proud and strident, hateful of the Spanish rape of their ancient nation and the invasions of other foreign forces, challenged Castillian domination.

In this resurgence of Mexican culture, artists glorified the mysteries of pre-Conquest America. Film directors made movies with actresses who had dark hair and *indígena* features. Federal attorneys found the prosecution of corrupt millionaires to be a stepping stone to political recognition by the Mexican people.

The Castillians struck back at the people of Mexico with the traditional weapons of Latin oligarchies: corruption and deceit.

The elite, in their demand for power to ensure wealth and privilege, had through the centuries developed corruption to an art. They instinctively knew the formulas for determining, at what price and in what circumstances, gold or dollars would break an oath of office.

They knew the techniques of the invisible manipulation of local officials.

They knew when to apply dollars and when to apply violence.

As the term of President Escheverria ended, hundreds of millions of dollars in bribes ensured the nomination and election of a new leader faithful to Castillian traditions.

Though the administration of President Lopez Portillo appeared to continue Escheverria's policy of promoting Mexican nationalism, the new leaders only mouthed meaningless slogans. These new leaders—who bragged of their pure geneology dating back to the Conquest, born into privilege, with Castillian names—blatantly exploited the nationalistic prejudices and misconceptions of the Mexican people by condemning the United States for its wealth and history of dominating the nations of Central and South America.

Simultaneous with their campaigns of denunciation of the United States, and of NATO and world capitalism, the Lopez Portillo Administration received a gift from deep beneath the rich soil of Mexico.

Oil.

President Portillo launched an ambitious national development program. But the president declared that petrodollars could not fund the creation of a socialist state as quickly as he wished.

With the oil beneath Mexico as collateral, the Lopez Portillo regime borrowed billions of dollars from American and European banks to finance the development of Mexico.

But these billions of dollars never reached the people of Mexico.

The wealthy elite became even more fabulously wealthy. Banks in the United States and Europe reported year after year of record deposits as Mexican leaders looted their nation.

But when the price of oil fell, when Mexico no longer had the flow of petrodollars to meet the interest payments, the orgy of greed ended.

Inflation attacked the value of the peso. The price of corn and beans, the staple foods of the common people, doubled then doubled again. Campesinos by the millions went north to work in the fields and factories of the United States.

In the cities of Mexico, mobs demanded an accounting of the stolen billions.

Leaving the crisis to his newly elected successor, President Lopez Portillo retired to his fifty-million-dollar mansion outside Mexico City. In a final ceremony, the departing president stood before the Mexican senate and accepted the praise and applause of the elite of Mexico. For he had already set in motion something that would buttress the fortunes of the Castillians through the years of his successors. He had begun the resurrection of the heroin syndicates of the sixties and early seventies.

Castillian wealth and privilege had been secured again.

And as had happened many times in Mexican history, foreign invaders once more came to the ancient land.

But these new invaders did not journey from Europe or North America. The elite of Mexico had found their allies among the criminals of El Salvador, Argentina and Chile.

Unlike the other invaders of Mexico, the fascists of the International came by invitation.

And Able Team came, the last invaders, because they damn well gave themselves no other choice.

10

In a storeroom of the abandoned garage, Vato prepared a drug. Gunther lay lashed to the springs of an iron bed, ropes securing his arms and legs and torso. He and the men of Able Team watched as Vato took the ingredients from a leather pouch, black with age and handling.

Vato put the knot of a cactus button on a board and chopped it with a knife.

"You think peyote will make me talk?" Gunther asked.

"This is not peyote."

"I am not unfamiliar with Mexico. I know what that is. I know I will not talk. You will only make me sick."

"It is like peyote, but it is not." Vato smiled to the prisoner. "You will soon know the difference."

An old porcelain cup and a rusty auto valve served as a mortar and pestle. After cutting the cactus button to hundreds of fine bits, he dropped it into the cup and crumbled in another substance. He ground the mixture to a powder. He added pinches of other powders. Then he took a folded square of paper from the pouch. The paper contained dried beetles the size of dimes.

"What do you call those?" Lyons asked.

Vato smiled and shook his head. He would not reveal the secrets. He dropped two of the beetles into the cup. Their shells crackled under the pestle as Vato ground them into the mixture.

Gadgets turned to their prisoner. "Last chance, colon-el. Talk now and you won't have to eat that crazy shit."

"It will do nothing!" Gunther declared. He glanced around the circle of onlookers.

His eyes met Coral's for a long moment.

Then Gunther laid his head back on the squeaking bed. He closed his eyes against the searing light of the bare bulb hanging from the ceiling.

A couple of tar-colored lumps went into the cup next. Vato pressed down hard, grinding and blending. He worked patiently, stopping from time to time to stir the mixture with his knife blade, then grinding again. When the mixture became a homogenous green-black dust, he tasted it and nodded.

"Hold his head," he told the others. "Open his mouth and pinch his nose shut. Kino, you pour the water."

Lyons and Blancanales immobilized Gunther's head while Gadgets tried to pull his jaw open. Gunther locked his jaw shut.

"Relax," Gadgets told him. "Some people pay money to take drugs."

Gunther struggled against Gadgets's hands. Glancing to his partners, Gadgets asked, "Was it because I didn't say please? Come on, open up. We gave you the chance to talk. Please, open up.... You're not cooperating—"

Gadgets slammed his fist into the side of Gunther's

head, using the full force of his arm to drive the knob of his center knuckle precisely into muscles and nerves over the sphenoid bone of Gunther's temple. A second blow struck the ropes of muscle over the condyloid process of the jaw.

Stunned, his jaw numb, Gunther could not resist as Gadgets pulled his mouth open.

Vato dropped in the powder. Gunther strained to twist his head. Kino carefully poured a stream of water down Gunther's throat. Gunther had to swallow or drown.

"Now we wait."

The effects came slowly. After thirty minutes, Gunther began to blink his eyes and shake his head from side to side. He breathed deeply. Lyons leaned over Gunther and saw that his eyes no longer focused.

Gunther's breathing came in rasps. Then his eyes closed. Vato grasped his wrist and counted his pulse rate. Vato nodded.

"Question him now."

"Who are you?" Blancanales asked in English.

Violence seized Gunther. Arching his back, all the tendons of his neck standing out like cables, he strained to break the rope that bound him to the iron bed. His body trembled, sweat streamed from his face. He gulped air in panting gasps.

Vato studied the reactions, then took a plastic kit from his drug bag. The kit contained a vial and a disposable syringe still in the plastic envelope. Vato assembled the syringe and put the needle into the vial.

"This will calm him."

"What is it?" Blancanales asked.

"Morphine."

"Don't put him to sleep!"

"He will not sleep for days." Vato injected a few milliliters of the narcotic.

The spasms stopped but Gunther continued struggling. Blancanales leaned over him and asked him in Spanish, *"¿Quién es?"*

Gunther raved through the night.

LYONS AND TWO OF THE YAQUI TEENAGERS, Kino and Jacom, stood guard on the rooftop. They alternated shifts, sleeping and watching the dark street. Cars and trucks sped by, bouncing over the broken pavement. People walked past without a glance at the abandoned garage. The street noises, the jets roaring overhead, the radios and televisions covered the screams and shouts of Gunther's delirium in the storeroom.

After midnight, the neighborhood fell quiet as the thousands of families in the tenements finally slept. But the sounds of the city never stopped, the traffic noise of the avenues and expressways still going on, planes and trucks and unmuffled motorcycles hurtling unseen through the gray, polluted night.

Despite the tropical latitude, Lyons shivered. He clutched his sports jacket tight around himself. At the elevation of Mexico City, more than two thousand meters above sea level, the air became cool after sunset. Now, in the predawn hours, the few people still on the streets wore jackets and sweaters.

He stared up at the flashing Tecate sign, a neon explosion of red and yellow letters framed in a blue afterimage against the gray night. Able Team had gone from searing desert to the tropical coast to the cool mountains in only a few days. His body had not time to acclimatize to the sudden changes. He said aloud, "I do get around. No doubt about it."

"*¿Qué es?*" Jacom asked.

"*Nada.*" Lyons knew the word because Gadgets used it often. He tried to explain that he had only talked to himself. "*Hablo…hablo nada.*" He didn't know enough Spanish to explain. He pointed down and left the rooftop.

Going down the steel stairs, Lyons heard an incomprehensible monologue of some guttural language. He saw Blancanales and Coral sitting by the bed, listening and taking notes. The fascist colonel thrashed against the rope restraints, his body soaked in sweat, his blind eyes snapping from side to side but never focusing.

Gadgets had electronic gear spread out on a table. He changed the cassette in the tape unit recording Gunther, then returned to the circuits of the NSA radios captured from the International. Lyons looked over his partner's shoulder. Gadgets pointed to the maze of circuits and components.

"I think they did a directional scan on this radio. That's how they got us on the freeway. Like a DF, except—"

"You deactivated it?"

"That's not it," Gadgets explained. "I think the encrypting generates a distinctive electronic signature. Apparently they picked up the signal. That's why one of their officers asked who was on the freeway. When no one answered, they sent some cars to check it out."

"So we can't monitor the Nazis now?"

"I wouldn't risk it. I guess we've lost that trick. Too bad. It was slick."

"But we got him talking," Lyons commented, looking at Gunther.

"It's a fact." Gadgets nodded. "That dope opened up the doors of his head. Problem is, we don't know what came out."

"What?"

Blancanales answered. He pointed to his pages of notes. "We can understand his Spanish and English. But he lapses in and out of German."

"You get a location? Names? Places?"

"No address." Blancanales shook his head. "Names and places and scenes. All flashbacks. But we can't ask him questions. He doesn't even know we're here—"

"Whatever Vatoman made," Gadgets added, "that stuff is rough."

"You mean we dragged this Nazi across a thousand miles of Mexico and we can't get the information?"

"Be cool!" Gadgets tapped a stack of cassettes. "I think we got something interesting here. It's a mystery, but it's a very, very interesting mystery."

Lyons snorted with bitter frustration. "We didn't come here to play Agatha Christie. We're here to find and destroy."

"Patience," Blancanales said. "We'll relay all these tapes to Stony Man. They can do the translation. We'll continue the search until—"

"We can't," Lyons told his partners. "The International has people in the DEA and the NSA. If we report to Stony Man, the International will monitor it all.''

"Don't sweat it, hardguy." Gadgets looked at Coral. "Miguel knows this city. We came up with a cool scam. No embassy contact, no trip to the DEA office, no satellite interlock. Simple, direct.''

"What?"

"We just call home.''

As the pilot guided the Piper Cub through the still morning air, Lieutenant Soto scanned the forested hills. The optics of his binoculars compressed the distances and perspective, reducing the misted landscape to patterns of green and gray and black. He focused on the rectangles of fields and pastures—any clearing larger than fifteen meters, the diameter of a UH-1 troopship's rotor blades.

But he saw no helicopter.

The lieutenant had received the report of the unauthorized helicopter the afternoon before. After calling the army units in the region to check the information, he had flown to Mexico City with two platoons of his soldiers. Now his soldiers waited in trucks while he circled in the spotter plane.

Again the helicopter eluded him.

This time, however, he had a confirmed sighting. An ex-air force officer, working on his ranch in the mountains, had seen it. The helicopter passed so close to him that he'd seen Mexican soldiers and North Americans riding inside with rifles in their hands. The retired officer had even noted that the doors of the troopship had been removed. The of-

HE'S EXPLOSIVE.
HE'S MACK BOLAN...
AGAINST ALL ODDS

He learned his deadly skills in Vietnam...then put them to good use by destroying the Mafia in a blazing one-man war. Now **Mack Bolan** ventures further into the cold to take on his deadliest challenge yet— the KGB's worldwide terror machine.

Follow the lone warrior on his exciting new missions...and get ready for more nonstop action from his high-powered combat teams: **Able Team**—Bolan's famous Death Squad—battling urban savagery too brutal and volatile for regular law enforcement. And **Phoenix Force**—five extraordinary warriors handpicked by Bolan to fight the dirtiest of antiterrorist wars, blazing into even greater danger.

Fight alongside these three courageous forces for freedom in all-new action-packed novels! Travel to the gloomy depths of the cold Atlantic, the scorching sands of the Sahara, and the desolate Russian plains. You'll feel the pressure and excitement building page after page, with nonstop action that keeps you enthralled until the explosive conclusion!

Now you can have all the new Gold Eagle novels delivered right to your home!

You won't want to miss a single one of these exciting new action-adventures. And you don't have to! Just fill out and mail the card at right, and we'll enter your name in the Gold Eagle home subscription plan. You'll then receive six brand-new action-packed Gold Eagle books every other month, delivered right to your home! You'll get two Mack Bolan novels, one Able Team and one Phoenix Force, plus one book each from two thrilling, new Gold Eagle libraries, **SOBs** and **Track**. In **SOBs** you'll meet the legendary team of mercenary warriors who fight for justice and win. **Track** features a military and weapons genius on a mission to stop a maniac whose dream is everybody's worst nightmare. Only Track stands between us and nuclear hell!

FREE! The New War Book and Mack Bolan bumper sticker.

As soon as we receive your card we'll rush you the long-awaited New War Book and Mack Bolan bumper sticker—both ABSOLUTELY FREE with your first six Gold Eagle novels.

The New War Book is *packed* with exciting information for Bolan fans: a revealing look at the hero's life...two new short stories...book character biographies...even a combat catalog describing weapons used in the novels! The New War Book is a special collector's item you'll want to read again and again. And it's yours FREE when you mail your card!

Of course, you're under no obligation to buy anything. Your first six books come on a 10-day free trial—if you're not thrilled with them, just return them and owe nothing. The New War Book and bumper sticker are yours to keep, FREE!

Don't miss a single one of these thrilling novels...mail the card now, while you're thinking about it.

GET THE NEW WAR BOOK AND
BUMPER STICKER
FREE! See exciting details inside.

ficer, suspicious because of the North Americans with the Mexican soldiers, reported what he saw.

No one else had reported the helicopter. The night before, the lieutenant had alerted all the police in the area. He had expected any information immediately.

Then came the killings on the Viaducto....

The lieutenant did not believe the events to be only coincidental. Mexicans and North Americans, in a stolen Mexican army helicopter, with automatic rifles, had been sighted in the mountains outside the capital. That same night, Mexicans and North Americans had killed other Mexicans and foreigners on an expressway in the city.

Lieutenant Soto had pledged himself to break this mystery. He would not fail.

LYONS WATCHED BLANCANALES AND GADGETS enter the Oficina de Teléfonos Larga Distancia. Sharing the first floor of the side-street office building with a bank, the oficina offered long-distance telephone and telegraph services to walk-in customers.

No equivalent commercial service existed in the United States, nor did it need to. In the States, every desk and table and kitchen wall features a telephone. It is not necessary to leave the house to place a long-distance call or to send a telegram. But in Mexico, a developing nation, the telephone companies cannot yet provide that universal telephone service. Nor can the companies ensure dependable service. The people of Mexico City tell a joke. "Want to talk to a stranger? Telephone a friend."

Coral explained that the Oficina assured correct

connections for personal and business calls. Every office featured working, static-free telephones and long-distance lines, and—important to Able Team—private booths, each with a chair and a writing table.

"There will be no problems," Coral assured them. He had taken the address of a long-distance office from the telephone book and given them directions. Coral stayed to sleep. He had sat with Blancanales beside Gunther all night, taking notes and recording his monologue. Coral would catch up on his sleep while the North Americans posed as businessmen relaying the recordings of their important meetings to their headquarters.

Now Lyons and Vato sat in one of the rented tourist cars, watching the street. Lyons held his fourteen-inch Atchisson under a newspaper. Vato concealed the sawed-off Remington in a flight bag. Ahead, Jacom waited behind the wheel of the other compact, an Uzi near his right hand. They took no chances, despite Coral's assurances. If the NSA monitored the Stony Man telephone lines, the international would know of the call from Mexico City before Gadgets switched off his tape player.

Blancanales and Gadgets talked with a clerk at the counter. Through the plate-glass windows, Lyons watched his partners give the clerk a slip of paper. The clerk pointed. They went to a booth.

On the street, a Mexican in a gray business suit approached the parked tourist car. The middle-aged man, dapper, gray haired, carried a briefcase and an umbrella. Lyons watched the man. Several manufacturers of submachine guns offered briefcase adaptations of their weapons. The dapper Mexican businessman would pass within an arm's distance of Lyons. Lyons turned to Vato.

"Can you go to the other side of the street? And watch there?" Lyons pointed to the shadowed doorways opposite the telephone office.

Vato nodded. Taking his flight bag, he left the compact car. He jogged through the early-morning brilliance and slipped into a doorway.

A step away from Lyons, the businessman stopped. Lyons watched the hand that gripped the briefcase handle as he slid his own hand under his coat. He wore his modified-for-silence Colt Government Model in a shoulder holster under his left arm. He touched the pistol's checked plastic grip.

The businessman put his umbrella under his other arm and pulled out a handkerchief. He blew his nose, stuffed the handkerchief back in his coat pocket. He continued past Lyons.

Lyons opened the car door. He put the newspaper-covered Atchisson on the seat, then gathered up newspapers and a brightly colored tourist map of the city. Crossing the sidewalk to the entry of a travel bureau, he made a pretense of studying the ads of Mexican and European resorts displayed in the window. But he watched the street reflected in the plate glass. He held the newspapers and map under his left arm to cover the shape of the Colt holstered beneath his jacket.

A woman passed, a plastic-net shopping bag on one arm and her teenage daughter clutching the other. The girl glanced at Lyons, their eyes meeting for an instant, the girl averting hers when she saw the strange North American smiling at her. Her mother looked at Lyons and scowled. Lyons laughed out loud.

Across the street, Vato continually scanned the neighborhood. Lyons watched the Yaqui leader. The young man's eyes always moved—glancing to the traffic on the boulevard, watching a truck pass, studying a teenager who roared past on a motorcycle. Vato saw everything. Yet he appeared at ease, unconcerned with the passing people and cars, like a bored young man waiting for a shop to open. Vato had natural abilities, the gift of grace despite stress.

Footsteps behind Lyons interrupted his thoughts.

"Mr. American!" a voice called out. "Where do you want to go?"

Lyons took his hand out of his coat as an elderly travel agent motioned him to enter the office. "*Pase adelante, por favor*. We have a beautiful country. You have come to the correct place to arrange your tour of our natural wonders."

"No thank you, sir. Love your country, but I'm here on business. And I've got to get to it." Lyons walked away toward the windows of the telephone office. He saw Gadgets and Blancanales inside one of the booths. Continuing to the corner, he glanced down both directions on the boulevard.

Smog paled the brightness of the high-altitude morning to a dull glare. Like a tourist seeing the sights, Lyons stood with his hands in his pockets, looking around at the different architectural styles. He watched the people hurrying past on the wide sidewalk, searching their faces for the one wrong expression, one wrong glance. When cars and trucks turned from the boulevard to the side street, he gave every driver a quick look.

Lyons did not underestimate the International. The fascists had an efficient organization, with cunning and ruthless commanders, financed and aided by every right-wing regime in the hemisphere. Any one of the people walking past, any one of the passing cars could mean sudden death.

"Hey, hardguy!" Gadgets called out as he and Blancanales pushed through the door of the telephone office. "You waiting for someone?"

Vato had the second car in motion. Lyons threw open the door and stepped in. An instant later Jacom followed, Gadgets slamming the car door closed as the Yaqui teenager whipped into traffic.

"How did they do that so fast?" Vato asked Lyons. "They had several cassettes. And we stayed only twenty minutes."

"Screeching," Lyons replied. "High-speed transmission and recording. The Wizard plays the cassette at ten times normal speed. At the other end, they record at ten times normal speed. When they play it back at normal speed, the recording sounds normal."

"Oh." Vato nodded. "High technology."

"You got it. Otherwise, we wouldn't have made that call. No way we'd stay in one place for hours, playing tapes over the phone while the Nazis closed a circle around us."

Weaving through the traffic of the boulevards and expressways, circling and zigzagging through the streets to lose any surveillance units, the two cars took separate routes back to the garage. Vato, the ex-lowrider from Tucson, skidded to a stop in front of the rolling steel door first. Lyons slouched low in the seat as Vato sent the door up, then spun the tires as he raced the car inside.

Davis ran from the shadows, an M-16 rifle in his hands. Ixto jerked down the rolling door.

The DEA pilot shouted, "Coral's gone! He's gone to the Nazis. We got to get out of here before—"

"Calm down!" Lyons told him. "What're you talking about?"

"Coral's one of them. I heard a van start up and it was Coral. And he took Gunther with him. They'll be here—"

"When did he go?"

"Fifteen minutes ago, maybe twenty. He waited until we were both up on the roof, watching for you. Then he was gone."

A horn honked outside. The door clanked up again and the other rented car sped inside.

"Move it!" Lyons shouted to his partners. "Coral's one of them. Him and the colonel are gone."

Gadgets and Blancanales threw open their doors. Lyons heard Davis explaining the betrayal and escape. But the ex-LAPD detective did not listen to the details. He ran up the steel steps to gather his equipment. He had heard enough.

Fascist units, backed by corrupt forces of the Mexican army and police, would encircle the garage.

Once the circle of squads of gunmen and soldiers closed, no weapons, no high-tech electronics would break that circle.

The North Americans and the Yaquis would be trapped.

Outnumbered, outgunned.

Outlaws in a foreign city.

11

A suite of rooms overlooking the Paseo de la Reforma served as the communications office for the International.

The International, through a Canadian transnational corporation, owned the ultramodern Trans Americas S.A. tower. The data center and administrative offices occupied the top floors of the high rise. Banks, brokers and other international corporations leased hundreds of offices on the lower floors. The operations of those companies also required computers and telecommunications. The offices of the International seemed to be only one more data-processing center for a financial institution.

Microwave antennae provided satellite links with other International forces in the cities of Mexico and the hemisphere. Rows of electronic consoles processed incoming data and messages, automatically decoding and printing fold-sheets for the attention of a commander's staff. Technicians monitored the operation of the machines and maintained the flow of printouts to the offices on the penthouse floor of the tower.

In a high-security cubicle, a lieutenant took notes on a voice message from Washington, D.C. The voice of the North American radioing from an NSA office a continent away came from the decoding circuits like a machine speaking, metallic and disembodied.

"We did not tape all the transmitted information. But what we recorded, we will relay to your commander. A translation will follow."

"Excellent!" The lieutenant underlined a notation. "We have units in motion."

The metallic voice laughed. "You get them. We're tired of those hotshots running around making trouble. Get them."

LYONS WHIPPED THROUGH THE TURNS, the bumper of his compact sedan only a few steps behind the Mitsubishi van that Blancanales drove. Vato led in the first compact. On the long blocks between turns, Ixto watched the traffic behind them.

"El camión está allí," Ixto told him.

In the rearview mirror Lyons saw the gunmen following in a Ford pickup truck.

They came to a traffic circle. Lyons accelerated to close the gap behind the van. Cars and trucks sped around the monument at the center, weaving through the city buses. Someone ahead braked. Blancanales braked, Lyons smashed the bumpers together, then Blancanales veered to the right. Lyons hit the bumper again. The van sped away.

Swerving across the wide boulevard, Vato made a right turn, accelerated, then skidded through a left turn. Blancanales followed only seconds later. Ixto gripped the panic handle on the dashboard as Lyons skidded through a turn. The gunmen in the pickup tried to follow but sideswiped a bus. Another bus rear-ended the truck.

Pedestrians stared at the wild driving of the blond North American. A traffic cop put up a hand to stop the crazed tourist, but Lyons skidded around the officer—the cop's sky-blue uniform shirt flashing past the passenger window—and accelerated for another block. A hard right turn took them into the shaded streets around a park.

Lyons watched the traffic in his rearview mirror. He saw no truck.

Vato and Blancanales slowed. Lyons flashed his headlights to signal them. They did not risk using their hand-radios. If the International could detect the electronic signature of the decoding components, the transmissions would lead the surveillance units to them. Lyons pulled up parallel to Blancanales's van.

"Where do we go to get rid of that wreck?" Lyons asked, shouting across Ixto to Blancanales.

Squares of white adhesive tape matching the van's white paint covered the patterns of 9mm bullet holes. But the improvised patches and the smashed-out windows would not pass the inspection of police or investigators.

"The tourist section," Blancanales answered. "The Zona Rosa. Rent one there. Stay close."

"If I get any closer, I'll be parked in your back seat."

"Figure of speech...."

An hour later, they had another passenger van. They stopped on a side street and transferred the heavy trunks and suitcases of weapons to the new rental. They left the bullet-pocked rental there. Then they crossed the district to a restaurant and ate a leisurely lunch while Blancanales called landlords and commercial real-estate agencies throughout the metropolitan area.

Blancanales described himself as a Puerto Rican entrepreneur who needed warehouse space immediately. Agencies referred him to one office after another. Finally he made an appointment with a rental manager. Blancanales and Vato went together to examine the warehouses.

The others waited at one of the neighborhood parks. Lyons watched old women walk babies in prams as Davis and the Yaquis tutored him in basic Spanish. As the hours passed, the nursemaids and small children left the park. Groups of shouting boys, in the white-shirt-and-black-pants uniform of a school, ran through the park, kicking a ball made of wadded paper in a plastic bag. Teenagers from another school walked through minutes later, boys with boys, girls in other groups, sweethearts two by two.

Finally, Blancanales and Vato returned. "We got a problem."

"Perros," Vato explained.

"Dogs in the warehouse?" Lyons asked.

Vato shook his head. He explained. *"Perros callejeros.* Street boys. They have nowhere to go. The manager said we must go get police to evict them."

Lyons shook his head. "No police. Pay the punks to leave if—"

"The problem's solved," Blancanales interrupted. "We told the boys we represented a government agency shipping cargo for the army. If they aren't gone when we get back, soldiers will throw them out.''

"And it just so happens we got four Mexican army soldiers, right?''

"It just so happens. . . .''

"THEY WORE THE UNIFORMS OF SOLDIERS, but they were not soldiers.''

Miguel Coral and Pedro Ramirez listened to Rico describe his eviction. Homeless for years, Rico survived on the streets by shining shoes. He slept where he could, in doorways, in alleys, or in abandoned buildings. He wore sandals and torn pants and a stained sweat shirt. Street filth crusted his skin. Shoe blacking stained his hands.

As a shoeshine boy, he listened as he worked. Often he heard important information. Men talked while boys shined their shoes, thinking the boys did not understand. But Rico understood the value of information. He had learned to listen and watch and remember. Today, he had heard of the reward for information on the North Americans who traveled with soldiers. He had talked with all his friends, all the people he knew from the streets. And then the North Americans had come, had actually appeared at the place where he and many other boys stayed.

"They wanted to rent the warehouse. Many of us are there and the Mexican says he will call the police. Then one of the other ones, he tells us—''

"This was the Puerto Rican?''

"Yes, the old one. The other one was young. He came back dressed like a soldier, the young one. The other one acted like a boss, telling the soldiers to move us out. All of them shout and say they will shoot us, so we went. That is when I saw the gringos outside. A blond one. And two others, North Americans.''

"Here—" Coral slid a sheet of paper and a pen to the boy "—draw the place.''

Across the table from the older men, Rico sat on his shoeshine kit and carefully sketched the outlines of and entries to the warehouse.

A television blared in the next room. Below the windows of the apartment, traffic rushed through the narrow street, horns sounding, brakes squealing. Ramirez, middle-aged like Coral, wore bifocal glasses to study the map Rico drew.

"How much will you pay me?''

Coral took a thousand-peso note from his pocket. He put it in front of the boy. Rico shook his head.

"One thousand is nothing for this. This is very important. I know. They said they were soldiers and they had machine guns and they were with North Americans. Maybe they are drug smugglers. Maybe they are terrorists. I want a thousand dollars.''

"You what?" Ramirez sputtered, astounded by the shoeshine boy's demand.

"If they are there,'' Coral told him, "we will pay another thousand. Pesos.''

"They are there!" Rico protested. "One hour ago, they were there. I come here. They are still there.''

"You say. When we see, we will be sure.'' Coral took out another five hundred pesos. "Here. Fifteen hundred. That is good pay. Now get their names.''

"I want dollars!"

Coral shook his head. "Boy, for dollars, you must bring me the men.''

"I will get their names!" Rico grabbed the money. He folded the bills and put them in a secret money pocket he wore. "I will go back and listen at the windows."

"Good," Ramirez told him. "Go, watch them. We will send men soon to watch. Tell them what you see, what the North Americans and soldiers do. My men will pay you a few dollars."

Rico ran down the stairs to the crowded sidewalk. Pushing through the crowds, he ran to the corner and jumped on a bus. But he did not return to the warehouse.

Why waste his time for pesos? The two old men of the Ochoas had paid him only fifteen hundred pesos. Rico knew others who would buy information about criminals pretending to be soldiers of the Mexican army.

Rico would sell the information again.

This time, he would demand dollars or stay silent.

"A THOUSAND DOLLARS?" the sergeant asked, not believing the ragged boy who stood at the door to his apartment.

"I know something very important. About some gringos and Mexican soldiers. They have money and machine guns."

"Soldiers? Machine guns?"

"Maybe they are the ones from the Viaducto. If you pay me, I will take you to them."

"I don't have that money." The sergeant considered the problem. He motioned the boy to step in. "But I will call my unit...."

"Tell them I want dollars."

"Don't we all?"

WALLS OF OFFICE LIGHTS towered above the street. As the gray evening became night, workers from the buildings crowded the sidewalks. Junior executives talked with young women in color-coordinated corporate uniforms. Buses stopped, the workers surging in through the doors. Others strolled toward the subway station two blocks away, talking to one another, buying newspapers and magazines from the newsstands lining the boulevard.

Across the street, in the circular driveway of a flashy hotel, taxis vied for tourist fares. Lyons watched as a blond, sunburned European argued with a taxi driver. The tourist pointed to the black hood covering the meter. The driver shook his head. He whistled to a traffic cop. The city policeman, then a hotel doorman joined the argument.

Lyons stood in a doorway a few steps from the entry to a long-distance telephone office. As he had that morning, he held newspapers and a tourist map under his left armpit to cover the unmistakable shape of his shoulder-holstered Colt. Vato and Jacom circled in the rented cars. Police standing on the corners did not allow any parking.

Inside the telephone office, Gadgets and Blancanales called Stony Man. Lyons could not see them from where he stood. But he had an unobstructed view of the entry and the street in front. In a few minutes, after Gadgets recorded the coded reply from Stony Man, Able Team would have the translation and evaluation of Gunther's ravings.

They needed an address, the name of a building. Somewhere in the recordings of the fascist colonel's drug delirium, there had to be a key.

Vato passed in one of the rented cars. He did not look at Lyons, but Lyons knew that Vato had scanned the telephone office and the street as he passed.

Headlights flashed across the sidewalk and a heavy Chevrolet pulled to the curb. Lyons stepped back into the doorway, taking his hand-radio from his coat pocket. He counted four wide-shouldered men inside. They looked through the windows of the telephone office. Lyons watched the Chevrolet, his thumb on the radio's transmit key. He would not risk betraying their location until he knew. . . .

One man pointed. Then three men threw open the doors of the Chevy and rushed toward the telephone office. One man stood at the entry, watching the sidewalk. As the other two went inside, their right hands going to shoulder-holstered pistols, Lyons hissed into the radio.

"Nazis! They're—"

A woman screamed. Noises. People on the sidewalk stopped. The gunman stationed at the door turned and looked inside. Gadgets's voice called from Lyons's radio.

"Hold them! We haven't got it all yet. Can you?"

"They're already in there."

"The two that ran in here? They are past tense."

"How much longer?"

A full-powered Detroit engine roared as another Chevrolet slipped around the corner. The driver skidded the car to a stop in front of the telephone office. Three more gunmen ran for the entry, Uzis in their hands. The people on the sidewalks scattered.

Bursts of autofire shattered the evening. A plate-glass window fell onto the sidewalk.

Going to one knee, Lyons gripped his Colt Government Model in both hands. He lined up the sights on the driver of the first Chevrolet, checked the sidewalk for bystanders, then squeezed off a silenced shot.

Blood splashed the inside of the windshield. The driver slumped over the steering wheel, the engine screaming with frenzied rpm as the dead man's foot pressed down the accelerator. Then the driver fell sideways onto the transmission lever.

Tires smoking, the Chevy raced backward, shearing off two doors of a parked taxi. The out-of-control sedan continued backward into the wide boulevard, scraped off a car's taillights and smashed into the side of a bus. Hundreds of cars skidded to a stop.

Sprinting from the doorway, Lyons ran for the other car. He saw the driver turning in the front seat, his hand coming up with an automatic. Lyons sidestepped to the left and the driver fired, the back windshield of the Chevrolet suddenly fracture-white, the 9mm slug passing high over Lyons's head.

A silent 3-shot burst of .45-caliber slugs from Lyons punched holes in the crystals of broken glass, the impacts of the hollowpoints like hammers slamming the dashboard. He continued around the Chevrolet and fired again, point-blank through the driver's window. Three more hollowpoints tore into the wounded man. Lyons reached inside and took the keys from the ignition.

An Uzi fired a last burst. Lyons ran toward the telephone office and looked inside. Dead men sprawled everywhere. A woman ran from the front doors, screaming, tottering on her high heels. Gadgets and Blancanales followed her out. Blancanales held his Beretta 93-R autopistol in a two-hand grip. Gadgets had his bag of gear in one hand, an Uzi in the other. Another Uzi hung on his shoulder.

A shotgun boomed. A block away, Lyons saw a muzzle flash twice, the cracks coming an instant later. Headlights wavered. A second pair of headlights accelerated from behind the first, and the shotgun fired again. Lyons heard a crash.

"Where are the cars?" Gadgets shouted.

"We'll take that one." Lyons ran toward the windshield-shattered Chevrolet and jerked open the door. He pulled the dead man out.

Another weapon fired somewhere on the next block. Lyons dropped to a crouch. But no bullets came. Listening for a moment, he heard no more shots, only blaring horns.

Vato's rental arrived, sliding sideways as it stopped. Vato held out Lyons's Atchisson with one hand, the forestock braced on the window trim. "There are many of them!" he shouted.

"Where's Jacom?"

"Back there, coming. Get in!"

"Take them." Lyons pointed to his partners. "I'll wait for Jacom."

Lyons pulled his Atchisson out of Vato's car window. Vato passed him another 7-round box-mag of 12-gauge shells as Blancanales and Gadgets got out of the Chevrolet and into the small car. Gadgets leaned across the back seat and pushed the door open.

"Get in! What're you waiting for?"

"Jacom! Where is he?" Lyons crouchwalked into

the open, the muzzle of the Atchisson straight up as he scanned the street for the Yaqui teenager. "I'm not leaving him here—"

"He's coming!" Vato told him. "Look back there."

The headlights of a compact flashed to high beam twice. Jacom waved from the window. Only then did Lyons get in the car with his partners.

"Move it!" Lyons pointed the Atchisson out the window, watching for any other gunmen of the International.

Vato stood on the accelerator, swerving past a bus, whipping the compact through a skidding right turn. Lyons looked back, saw Jacom following them.

"We made it. . . . What did Stony Man tell you?"

Gadgets shook his head with disbelief. "This is all too weird. Gunther isn't a Nazi, he's—"

Veering across three lanes of traffic, a pickup closed on them. A gunman stood up in the back and raised an Uzi.

A blast from the Atchisson flipped him backward from the truck. Lyons turned in the seat and sighted on the driver.

The truck swerved, headlights glaring through the back window of their rental car, then accelerated, the driver reaching out the window to point a revolver.

Firing point-blank, Gadgets killed the driver with a captured Uzi, the long burst throwing the driver sideways into another man, his hand pulling the wheel hard to the right. Gadgets fired until the bolt slammed down on the empty chamber. The truck went over the curb and into a sidewalk vending booth. Newspapers and magazines exploded into the air.

Gadgets dropped the empty Uzi to the pavement, the weapon clattering end-over-end on the asphalt.

"Gunther's what?" Lyons asked.

"He made all that noise we thought was German?"

"Yeah, yeah. What was it?"

"German. And Russian. He's an East German. KGB."

Headlights wove through the traffic. Muzzles flashed with autofire.

12

Pointing to a doorway, Lieutenant Soto posted two of his soldiers to watch the street. Then the lieutenant led his platoon into the darkness. They wore black fatigues and neoprene-soled boots. Wax stick blacking darkened their faces. Tape on the stocks of their M-16 rifles eliminated noise.

As silent as a shadow, the line of twenty soldiers moved through the darkness of the alley.

The lieutenant walked slowly, gently pushing aside trash with his boots before he eased down his weight. He flicked his eyes from side to side. He scanned the doorways, the warehouse loading docks, the mounds of paper and plastics.

Rats ran through the filth and trash piled behind the warehouses. Cans rattled. A block away, a diesel truck roared through its gears. From time to time, workers in one of the factories hammered sheet metal, the banging echoing through the alley. The lieutenant picked up the pace. None of the foreigners in the warehouse would hear the small sounds of the soldiers' soft-soled boots on the asphalt.

The shoeshine boy had described the men. The Mexicans who had impersonated soldiers matched the descriptions of the soldiers accompanying the mysterious helicopter. The lieutenant had not matched the boy's descriptions of the North Americans to those of any known criminals. But tonight he would interrogate the foreigners.

If they surrendered.

If they did not, the lieutenant would send morgue photos to North America and Europe.

There would be no escape this time. A platoon of soldiers, headed by his sergeant, watched the street entrance to the warehouse. The lieutenant and the second platoon now moved to secure the back exits. A few blocks away, an army colonel and a metropolitan police commander coordinated the action of the Mexican army antidrug unit with the patrols of the city police in the area.

Among the shadows and gray forms, Lieutenant Soto saw the ramp. That ramp led into the warehouse rented by the foreigners. A line of yellow light under the warehouse door indicated activity inside.

The lieutenant tapped the chests of the two soldiers behind him, then pointed to a doorway. The soldiers silently took positions in the shadows. A few steps farther, the lieutenant sent two more soldiers to creep into the space between two buildings. Other soldiers walked up a flight of concrete steps to a loading platform. They went prone.

After dispersing his men in groups of two and four to positions opposite the warehouse, the lieutenant finally keyed his walkie-talkie. He wore the small radio on the shoulder strap of his web gear, the case secured by a strip of Velcro. He whispered into the microphone.

"We are ready. You see anything?"

"Nothing," the sergeant answered. "The beggar boy might have lied."

"We will know soon. I am entering the building now."

Clicking off the transmit key, Lieutenant Soto slipped across the alley.

BULLETS SLAMMED SHEET METAL, then an explosion of tiny cubes of tempered glass filled the interior of the rental compact. A bullet had smashed out the back window and continued on to spider-shatter the windshield. Lyons turned in the back seat. Smashing out the shards of fracture-patterned glass with the short barrel of his assault shotgun, he pointed the Atchisson at the pursuing car.

He aimed above the left headlight of the swerving, speeding car and fired, but an instant too late. The number-two and double-ought steel shot tore away the driver's side mirror and shattered the window. The driver whipped the steering wheel in the opposite direction, the tires screaming across the wide boulevard. Sideswiping a delivery van, the sedan accelerated to parallel Able Team's compact. Two gunmen pointed Uzis out the right side windows to strafe Able Team.

Jacom accelerated from behind the sedan. He pointed a Mini-Uzi out his window and fired one-handed, the machine pistol spraying a 30-round magazine in a fraction of a second, slugs breaking windows, hammering sheet metal. As the gunmen swiveled to return the fire, Jacom hit the brakes and turned to the left, putting his car behind the sedan.

The distraction gave Lyons time to plan his shots.

He lined up the white tritium dots of his Atchisson on the front passenger-side window of the sedan and fired. Steel shot tore metal and flesh. The impact threw the gunman in the passenger seat against the driver. Lyons fired through the window again and again, until the assault shotgun's bolt locked back.

Wheel rims shrieked against concrete. The doomed car jumped the curb and plowed into the marble base of a monument. Glass and chrome flew everywhere.

Whipping his small car past the wreck, Jacom accelerated and closed the gap between the two compacts. He flashed his high beams, then Vato powered Able Team's car through a skidding left-hand turn, then a right. He leaned on the horn to speed through a neighborhood, Jacom only a car's length behind him.

Lyons kept his Atchisson below the level of the windows.

"They were most definitely monitoring," Gadgets told his partners. "This morning, too, I'll bet."

"No more calls home." Lyons changed Atchisson mags. He propped the selective-fire assault against the door and unholstered his silenced Colt. He cleared the chamber, then jammed in another standard-issue 7-round magazine.

"And that means they know what we know," Blancanales added. "They'll know exactly what we got from Gunther and what we didn't. If there's an address on the tape, they'll be gone tomorrow."

Lyons looked at his watch. "Tomorrow's four hours away."

"It'll take me that long to go through these

tapes!'' Gadgets protested. ''I can't decode it in a flash, you know.''

''Then get with it now,'' Lyons said.

Gadgets snapped a salute. ''Yes, sir. Immediately. Switching into target-acquisition mode.''

As Vato drove back to the warehouse, Gadgets put on miniature headphones and skipped through the tapes. ''Wow, man, this Gunther dude gets around. Chile, Argentina, El Salvador, Guatemala. Everywhere the Nazis hang out.''

''Where's he now?'' Lyons demanded. ''Forget the travelogue.''

''*Jawohl*, Herr Ironman! Working on it.''

Vato swerved through the narrow streets, speeding through the boulevard traffic, Jacom a car length behind him. Lyons watched for pursuit units. It looked as if they had lost the International.

In the industrial section, the compacts sped past factories and diesel trucks. Vato announced that they neared their rented warehouse. Lyons leaned forward.

''Don't go the front way. Circle around the block and then go in by the back alley.''

Vato nodded. He drove for a minute more, then turned into an alley. As he sped through the narrow lane, Vato hit the high beams. Lyons saw a shape dart into the shadows.

Throwing open the door, Lyons stepped out running. The black-clad form reached for a holstered pistol. Lyons dived. Breath exploded from a man's lungs as Lyons hit him, then locked a left arm around the man's throat. Lyons took the automatic from his prisoner's holster and put the muzzle against the man's head. He thumbed back the hammer and flicked up the safety.

Voices shouted. Forms blocked the alley. Flashlight beams found Lyons where he struggled with the soldier. Vato switched off the headlights as Blancanales ran to Lyons and crouched beside the prisoner.

"We're surrounded!" Blancanales yelled.

Forcing his prisoner flat on the concrete, Lyons pressed the muzzle of the battered Colt Government Model against the head of the soldier. "Who are you?"

"I am Lieutenant Soto of the army of the Republic of Mexico. You are under arrest. Surrender now, or you die."

"Cut the talk, Mexican. I got *you*."

"And he's got us," Blancanales added.

"You work for the International?" Lyons demanded.

"What?" the lieutenant asked.

"The Reich. The Nazis. The International Group. The Guerreros Blancos. Who are you with?"

"What do you talk about?"

Vato and Gadgets crouched behind the compact, their weapons ready. But they held their fire.

Two soldiers stopped Jacom, putting the muzzles of their M-16 rifles through the car's window. The Yaqui kept his hands on the steering wheel as one of the soldiers reached in and switched off the engine.

Gadgets called out to his partners. "It's a Mexican standoff!"

"Surrender or we kill you," the lieutenant threatened.

"Tough talk, Lieutenant," Lyons warned. "Any of your men shoot and you're gone."

"May I attempt to negotiate this problem?" Blancanales suggested.

"You are my prisoners," the lieutenant stated. "My sergeant has another twenty men watching the streets."

"Lieutenant," Blancanales said calmly, "there is a conspiracy operating within the Mexican army and various offices of the regional governments. This conspiracy also employs agents within the U.S. Drug Enforcement Agency. We are special antiterrorist operatives. We came to your country to participate in a bilateral investigation, and it's been one long fight. We fought a battalion of the Mexican army called the International Group. We fought *Federales*. We fought drug-syndicate gunmen. We'll cooperate with any legitimate Mexican authority, but you must recognize our problem. We've been tricked and betrayed by everyone, in your government and in ours. Is it possible you could call your commanding officer? I'm sure if we discuss this, we can resolve the situation."

"American antiterrorist operatives?"

"We came to investigate links between an international death squad, Los Guerreros Blancos, and the international drug syndicates."

"Did you have a helicopter?"

"We captured it from the Mexican army unit called the International Group."

The Lieutenant shouted out to his soldiers. *"¡No dispare! Esperan. Me dijeron que son agentos de anti-terrissimo de los Estados Unidos."* He turned to Blancanales. "Release me. We will talk. Remember, escape is not possible."

"Not for you!" Lyons countered.

"Release him," Blancanales instructed his partner. "But remember this," he said to the lieutenant, his voice rising. "We have been tricked by your government and ours. Betrayal is everywhere. Seriously, how do you expect us to take such insanity? You think we should just take this shit?" His eyes glared with fury and determination.

Lyons broke his lock around the lieutenant's throat. But he kept the man's automatic.

Lieutenant Soto spoke into his walkie-talkie. A voice answered. As the lieutenant whispered into the radio secured to his chest strap, the scene remained otherwise motionless.

The soldiers watched Able Team, Able Team watched the soldiers. No one risked a sudden move.

Finally, the lieutenant spoke to the foreigners again. "He will come."

Then he called to his soldiers. The two men pointing rifles at Jacom stepped away from the rental car. They took positions watching the foreigners. Soldiers blocked the other exit at the far end of the alley.

Lyons and Blancanales sat with Lieutenant Soto on the truck ramp. The headlights of the rented cars lit the scene. Blancanales used the wait to question the lieutenant.

"Your commander is a patriotic soldier?"

"*¡Claro que si!* Why do you ask such a question?"

"And as a senior officer, he earns a good salary, yes?"

"He is comfortable. Why do you—"

"Lieutenant, I do not mean to insult your commander. But I must ask. Has he become inexplicably more comfortable, even wealthy in the past year?''

"He says he has been successful in his investments.''

"He says?''

"I do not interrogate my commander.''

"And your sergeant. Is he a successful investor also?''

"No," the lieutenant laughed. "For a gift for his grandchild's baptism, he borrowed the money from me.''

"Could you perhaps ask the sergeant to watch the street? If anyone other than your commander appears, if the sergeant sees cars or trucks he does not recognize, could you ask him to notify you immediately? Please do not misunderstand me. But it is possible that anything is possible.''

The lieutenant nodded and spoke quickly into his walkie-talkie. A voice answered immediately. The lieutenant relayed the message to his captors.

"He sees many headlights.''

Lyons yelled, "Wizard! Jacom! Off the lights! Right now!''

Moving slowly, Gadgets set down his Uzi, then leaned into the car to switch off the headlight. The lights of the second car went black an instant later.

They heard engines. Tires squealed around corners. Blancanales spoke quickly to the lieutenant.

"Tell your soldiers to take cover! The International—''

"You are my prisoners, you don't give me commands!''

"Lieutenant! They are the enemies of your nation and ours! Your men will die if—"

Tires screeched to a halt. Autofire shattered the night. Bullets shrieked the length of the alley. A soldier screamed with pain.

Soldiers returned the fire. Other soldiers shouted to their lieutenant for instructions.

"We're on your side, Lieutenant," Lyons told the Mexican officer.

"Return my pistol!"

Lyons eased down the old Colt's hammer and passed it to the lieutenant.

Snapping back the hammer, Lieutenant Soto aimed at Lyons's face.

13

Autoweapons flashed, lighting the alley like strobes. A single tracer streaked across the darkness, sparked against a wall, spun wildly into the night.

Gadgets stayed flat on the asphalt. He heard a wounded man screaming. Slugs hammered the rented car, glass shattered and fell. Voices shouted Spanish. The wounded man called for his friends to help him, his words going from sobs to moans to cries for help again. Gadgets reached out and grabbed Vato's arm.

"What're they saying? What's going on?"

"The soldiers call the lieutenant. For instructions. The lieutenant calls for soldiers to take the prisoners. The gang tells them to run away, to leave the North Americans."

Gadgets shouted toward the warehouse ramp. "Pol! Ironman! Let the lieutenant go."

"I did! He's pointing a pistol at me."

"Silence!" Lieutenant Soto ordered.

Slinging his captured Uzi over his shoulder, Gadgets slipped out his Beretta 93-R. He touched the extractor to confirm a round in the chamber. Then he whispered to Vato.

"Count to ten, then switch on the car lights for an instant. Just an instant. On and off. Think you can do that without getting shot?"

"When the gang sees the lights—"

"I know, I can dig it. Instant target. Just on and off. I only need a millisecond of light."

"To free the others, yes?"

"That's the scam."

"Go."

"Just do it and get down. One!"

Counting to himself, Gadgets crept across the asphalt to the ramp. Before the firefight, he had seen Lyons and Blancanales with the Mexican lieutenant in the corner of the freight dock. Now he navigated by memory through the darkness. The shouts and shooting covered his steps.

His fingers found the concrete ramp. Paralleling the ramp, he continued to the spot where the ramp met the elevated loading dock. Kicking through litter, he heard Blancanales arguing with the lieutenant in an urgent whisper. Gadgets pointed the Beretta into the black.

The lights came on, Gadgets lining up the sights on the Mexican officer, the lieutenant turning, the muzzle of the Colt swinging around, Lyons moving, Blancanales shouting, "Don't kill him."

Darkness again. Then the Colt flashed, lighting the image of Lyons pushing the Colt up to the sky with his left hand as his right fist hit the lieutenant's jaw. Gadgets held the Beretta ready as he listened to Lyons disarm the Mexican.

"You punk," Lyons cursed. "You bozo excuse for soldier. Your men are getting killed and you won't talk sense. You just lost your command. Pol, tell those soldiers out there what to do."

"Can't do it. They wouldn't listen to me. He's

their officer. Lieutenant, may I suggest that you take us prisoner later?''

"You surrender?"

Lyons refused. "No way!"

Blancanales negotiated. "We'll continue talking after—"

Gadgets solved it. "Hey, Lieutenant. Our cars are shot to shit, we're on foot, we're in a strange city—how're we going to get away? Talking about surrender don't mean a thing. Because you got us."

"True," the lieutenant said. "And perhaps the other things you said are true. But there will be many questions. For you and whoever sent you into my country. Stay here."

They heard his boots hit asphalt. He called to a soldier. At the other end of the alley, weapons flashed, the gunmen firing when they heard the lieutenant's voice. Trash scattered, cans rolled.

"Whose side is he on?" Gadgets asked.

"He doesn't understand the situation," Blancanales answered.

"I do." Lyons dropped off the loading dock. Crabbing across the asphalt, slugs zipping through the night above him, he blundered into someone and banged into the car.

"Who is—"

"That you, Vato?"

"*Sí. Qué es*. . . . What is the problem?"

"Problem's over. Where's Jacom? Anything from Ixto or Davis or Kino?"

"Nothing from the others. Jacom is there." Vato pointed somewhere in the darkness. Lyons could not see his hand.

Then the night went white. The alley became a black-and-white scene of shifting forms and lines touched by bursts of red. The warehouses, the loading doors, a gunman running in the center of the alley—the scene and moving images oscillated as a searing white point of light above the alley swung on a tiny parachute.

In the flare light, the soldiers sprayed full-auto 5.56mm bullets at the running gunman. The cloth of his suit shook and rippled with the impacts of high-velocity slugs. A mist sprayed behind him, thousands of tiny drops glittering with magnesium white light. Dead in the air, the gunman never completed his stride.

"*¡Los otros!*" The lieutenant shouted again and again.

Soldiers aimed their weapons at the gunmen at the far end of the alley, where several sedans and pickups blocked the exit. The white glare exposed three gunmen in the open. Rifle fire from the platoon threw one man against a truck, spun another. The third man went flat behind a mound of trash. Bullets tossed bits of garbage into the air. Cans clanked and jumped.

Lyons took his Atchisson from the car. He took two full Atchisson mags from the floor and shook off the broken glass. The mags went in the left-hand pockets of his pants. Snapping back the cocking lever to chamber a round from the magazine in the weapon, he waited.

Tires skidded, headlights appeared at the other end of the alley as the International cut off any escape.

Lyons closed his eyes against the flare light and waited. The firing continued, the squads of gunmen targeting the soldiers.

Lyons waited with his eyes closed, breathing steadily, preparing himself for the sprint. He calmed himself despite the firing of the autoweapons and the screams and the shouting.

The alley went dark. Lyons dashed across the alley. He had almost no vision in the dark, but he heard other shoes running, then saw two shapes with Uzis. Lyons threw himself against a wall, stumbled through trash, found a doorway. The Uzis fired. The platoon replied with one long ragged burst, high-velocity slugs singing past the doorway, ricocheting from concrete and steel, a man grunting with the shock of a wound. Then the alley went white again.

A Mexican in a sports coat stood beside Lyons. As the Mexican brought up an Uzi, Lyons slammed him with the butt of the Atchisson. Stunned, the gunman fell back against a steel door. Lyons kicked the Mexican, driving a full-power karate front kick into the man's crotch. Gasping, falling forward, the gunman took another kick in the face.

Slugs tore past the doorway. Lyons untangled the Uzi from the semiconscious man's hands.

Hands grabbed him from the back. Lyons whipped around, swinging the Uzi in his left hand like a hammer.

A dying gunman, his clothes soaked in his blood, his nose and one eye gone, fell on Lyons. Lyons threw the blind man aside, then kicked him in the throat. The blind man clutched at Lyons's foot.

Scanning the alley for other fascists, Lyons smashed his shoe down on the gunman's throat, crushing his larynx. He died choking as Lyons stripped off his belt and used it to tie the hands of the first gunman.

Searching their pockets, Lyons found a revolver and spare Uzi mags. The revolver went in his coat pocket. He put a full mag in an Uzi. The Uzi in his left hand, his Atchisson in his right, Lyons crouched in the doorway, waiting as the flare swung lower and lower in the sky.

The alley went black. The fascists threw grenades into the darkness, the blasts coming in one ragged explosion. The fire from the soldiers stopped. A group of gunmen rushed past Lyons, their Uzis and sawed-off shotguns flashing. Lyons sprinted from the doorway.

A gunman crouching behind a sedan saw Lyons, but didn't fire. Like the fascists, Lyons wore slacks and a sports coat. The moment of hesitation cost the fascist his life. Point-blank, Lyons triggered a one-handed burst of 9mm bullets into the gunman's face.

As Lyons wove through the cars, another gunman turned toward him, with a bloody bandage on one arm, the other hand holding a pistol. A single blast from the Atchisson threw him back.

A bullet ripped past Lyons's head. He dropped and spun, his left hand spraying slugs.

Full-jacketed 9mm parabellums gouged car steel, broke glass, tore through the legs of a charging fascist. A slug shattered a femur, the leg bowing outward. The man went down screaming, clutching his twisted leg. Lyons put a 2-shot burst through the top of the fascist's head, and the Uzi's bolt slammed down on the empty chamber.

Another flare popped. Lyons crouched between the cars. He heard firing coming from the street. The cars and trucks blocked his view. He scanned the area around him, saw two gunmen with M-16 rifles climbing stairs to a warehouse roof. Lyons dropped out the spent Uzi mag, then jammed another into the Israeli machine pistol. He slung the weapon, letting it hang on his left side.

Putting the Atchisson to his shoulder, he sighted on the fascists going to the roof. A blast of double-ought and number-two steel shot threw one man against the concrete wall. The other man turned, took a storm of steel balls in the chest and face. Screaming, blood spraying from his torn lungs and throat, he fell back against the wall, lurched forward and finally fell over the railing. He screamed some more as he dropped to the street.

Footsteps pounded between the cars. Lyons heard the gunmen shouting to one another. He understood some of the panicked words.

A grenade bounced over the asphalt. Lyons kicked it away, heard it roll under the nearest car and continue beyond. Still crouching, he stepped up into the open door of the rental car.

The grenade flashed, thousands of tiny steel razors zipping under the parked vehicles, tires blowing, a man screaming. Another grenade bounced on sheet metal. This one fell next to the car in which Lyons hid.

Scrambling across the back seat, he saw a gunman standing in the back of a pickup. The gunman watched the space where Lyons had been. When the grenade banged, Lyons fired the Atchisson once, flipping the fascist backward.

A fireball rushed up into the night from the car's ruptured gas tank. Lyons ran from the flames. Forms moved in the orange light. Firing single shots, he dropped one after another. Then he rushed into the open, away from the jam of International vehicles.

A hundred meters away, muzzles flashed. High-velocity slugs zipped past Lyons. He dived, slamming into the sidewalk. Rolling, he hit a wall with his shoulder. Concrete steps blocked the rifle fire, slugs skipping off the steps and whining away. He looked up, saw a door. But the door had no handle. No escape that way. He looked back, saw fascists against the flames. Crisscrossing autofire went over him. He did not reveal his position by shooting. Pulling out the hand-radio in his coat pocket, he keyed the transmit.

"This is the Ironman. I'm on the street. Down behind some steps. I think I'm in a cross fire between the goon squad and the army."

In the alley, Gadgets answered first. "The lieutenant's taking it slow. Moving his men up. Looks to me like it's almost over."

"Get to him. Tell him to radio his sergeant that I'm one of the good guys."

"Will do." Gadgets left the cover of the bullet-riddled car. Staying low, he zigzagged across the alley. He crouched behind two soldiers. They reared back when they saw his sports coat and casual shirt, the uniform of the fascists. Gadgets put up his hands, the palms forward and open.

"Paz, amigos. Yo estoy a sus lado. ¿Dónde está el teniente?"

A soldier pointed to a freight door. *"Allí."*

Gadgets dashed to the lieutenant's position. *"¡No dispare!* Don't shoot," he called out. "Good guy coming. Lieutenant Soto?"

"Here. What is it?"

"My partner's up there, out on the street. He's caught between the goons and your other platoon. Could you radio your sergeant and tell him not to shoot him?"

"He's up there? He has joined the ones you say are the enemy?"

"Joined them to kill them. He rushed them, didn't you see? You think the Nazis threw those grenades at one another?" Gadgets pointed to the flaming cars and trucks. "Look at that. Death and destruction."

The lieutenant spoke into his walkie-talkie.

Against the steps, Lyons stayed low. He had put down his Atchisson. With his modified-for-silence Colt, he watched for fascist gunmen in the flames. More than silencing the pistol, the suppressor would also eliminate the muzzle-flash.

A silhouette went from one shadow to another. Squinting into the blazing gasoline, Lyons lined up the Colt's night-sight dots on the form. He saw the silhouette shift. Aiming at the curve suggesting the top of a head, Lyons squeezed off a shot.

The head moved, the gunman rising to fire at the advancing soldiers. The .45-caliber hollowpoint skipped off the hood of a car. Lyons saw a piece of the silhouette spin away.

A piercing, bubbling scream came from the wounded fascist. He rose to his feet and staggered. Lit by flames, the man clutched at his open throat and face, his hands searching for a jaw finding only a tongue and a vast wound. Then rifle fire threw him back.

Lyons saw another man crawling along the asphalt, dragging one leg. A .45 hollowpoint smashed through his other leg, flipping him onto his back. The fascist clawed at the street, trying to somehow escape the agony of his wounds.

Rifles continued to fire from the alley and from the other end of the street. But Lyons saw no more fascists with weapons. He keyed his hand-radio again.

"I think it's all over on this end."

Gadgets answered. "The lieutenant's going slow. Leapfrogging from door to door. Very cautious fellow. Not like some people we know."

Blancanales spoke next. "The other International unit's withdrawing. The cars are gone. Stay low until the soldiers find you. And cooperate, understand?"

"I always cooperate." Lyons clicked off, then muttered, "With people who know what they're doing."

Holstering his Colt, Lyons stayed in the shelter of the steps, listening to the soldiers shouting to one another. The platoon stayed a block away, firing single shots at movement in the flaming cars. But no fascists returned the fire.

The door above the steps opened. A flashlight blinded him. As his hand closed around the pistol-grip of his Atchisson, four hands grabbed Lyons's arms and coat and dragged him through the door. He felt his Atchisson torn away. He kicked and struggled, but other hands restrained him. Then knees on his chest and arms and legs immobilized him.

An electric light went on.

He looked up into the face of Miguel Coral.

14

Soldiers waved flashlights over the faces of dead men. Other soldiers collected weapons while medics tended to the wounded. Blancanales and Gadgets, accompanied by Lieutenant Soto, searched through the wreckage and corpses for Lyons. The hulks of the cars still burned, acrid black soot floating in the air, the fires casting an orange light over the street.

They found fascist gunmen killed by shotgun blasts, but Carl Lyons had disappeared.

Blancanales looked from the gutted cars to the long street. Thirty-odd meters away, concrete steps went from the sidewalk to a door. In the other direction from the fires, he saw no steps, only shallow doorways and the steel framing of stairs to the roof of a warehouse.

At both ends of the street, held back by soldiers and police, crowds of people stared at the scene. The lights of a television crew panned from soldier to soldier as the cameraman recorded video images for the news.

"That's got to be where." Gadgets pointed to the concrete stairs under the door.

"He didn't say 'doorway'?" Blancanales asked.

"Nah, man. 'Steps.' "

"What about that fire escape over there?"

"No cover. He wouldn't lie low there."

A soldier jogged up. *"Teniente Soto. Los otros han salido. No están—"*

Motioning the soldier to be silent, the lieutenant took him aside to hear his report. Gadgets and Blancanales walked to the concrete steps.

"He said the others had gone?" Gadgets asked Blancanales.

"That's it. But what others?"

"One mystery at a time...." Gadgets went up to the door and tried to push it open. Locked. Shining a penlight on the steps, he saw long scratches where bullets had scarred the concrete. He waved the penlight over the area.

Brass sparkled on the street's asphalt. Gadgets jumped off the steps and picked up a casing.

"Forty-five caliber. The man was here. But now he's gone."

"So he escaped?" the lieutenant asked as the North Americans rejoined him.

Blancanales shook his head. "He wouldn't have left us without telling us what he intended to do."

"Are you positive?" the lieutenant demanded.

"When the shooting started," Gadgets snapped at the lieutenant, "did you run away?"

"No!"

"Then neither did our partner."

"But the others ran away," the lieutenant said. "The ones inside the warehouse."

"The others?"

"The North American and the Mexicans. And the

ones who you left here escaped before we came. Also the two *indígenas* who drove your cars—now they are gone.''

Gadgets and Blancanales glanced at each other. Vato and Ixto had slipped away in the chaos of the firefight. And somehow Davis and Kino had spotted the surveillance and escaped before the army encircled the warehouse. The others did not have radios. They could not inform Able Team of their actions.

But Lyons did carry a radio.

GENERAL MENDEZ, commander of the Internacional de Mexico and the Grupo Internacionale del Ejercito Mexicano, reviewed the tapes of the intercepted communications. Alone in the penthouse office thirty floors above the Paseo de la Reforma, the general did not risk having anyone overhear the tapes. He listened to phrases in four languages inside his headphones.

The technical difficulties of the interception, and poor maintenance of the telephone line monitoring the transcontinental call, degraded the quality of the recording. Tape hiss and static distorted the voices, obscuring words and inflections. But he understood the German and Russian ravings of Colonel Gunther. And he also understood the English of the American technician speaking to his officer at the base in Virginia called Stony Man Farm.

The night before, the general had mobilized all available forces to search the capital of Mexico for the Americans. He had authorized his unit leaders to hire drug-syndicate gunmen as reinforcements. Other

International units, serving in the states of Sonora and Sinaloa, had received commands to return to Mexico City.

He had told his unit leaders that he would not accept failure. If they did not find and destroy the Americans, the leaders faced execution themselves. As an added incentive, he promised rewards to the units. One hundred thousand dollars for the freeing of Colonel Gunther; one hundred thousand dollars for the confirmed killing of an American; and two hundred fifty thousand dollars in gold to any officer of the International who succeeded not only in freeing Colonel Gunther, but also in capturing an American for interrogation.

Now, as the general listened to the tapes of the intercepted phone calls, units of the International battled with the Americans in the streets.

But after hearing the tapes, he dreaded the imminent victory. No longer did he view the Americans as a problem to the security of the International. The taped communications had altered his concerns. The communications threatened the general with death and the KGB with failure.

United in their conservatism and Castillian heritage, several countries in the Americas—El Salvador, Guatemala, Chile, Argentina—had contributed funds and soldiers to the cause of the International. The men fought in the belief they opposed the advance of Soviet communism.

But the Americans now knew that Colonel Gunther and General Mendez served the Soviet Union.

If captured by a unit of the International, the Americans would reveal the allegiance of the International's commander and the supposedly Paraguayan Colonel Gunther.

Perhaps General Mendez could explain away the story of KGB sponsorship of the International. Who would believe the truth? European and North American peaceniks denounced the armed forces of the conservative Pan-American nations as armies of fascist assassins. Voice of Moscow broadcasts labeled the governments of all Western Hemisphere nations—except Cuba and Nicaragua—as fascist regimes. The soldiers of the International would not believe they fought for the Soviet Union.

But what if the Americans played the tapes of Gunther's interrogation? What if International soldiers listened to the tapes and understood? What if the fantastic revelation started the soldiers questioning?

General Mendez armed his forces with weapons purchased on the international arms market—Israeli Uzis, American M-16 rifles, Belgian FN rifles. But some situations required more sophisticated weapons: explosives, or electronics, or antiarmor-antiaircraft rockets. Secrecy dictated a secure supply of high-quality weapons. The Soviet Union provided these weapons through intermediaries. The general then told his subordinates that he had purchased the Soviet ordnance from the Israelis, who had captured the matériel in Lebanon.

If an officer suspected the fascist-Soviet link, the officer might investigate. The simple procedure of matching the serial numbers of their weapons to the lists of serial numbers compiled by Israel after the

Lebanese invasion would reveal a discrepancy. Perhaps the general could explain that away also....

And perhaps not.

The general knew he must act immediately to end the risk. He keyed a code into the intercom. A minute later, the technician who had supervised the interception entered the penthouse office. Like General Mendez and Colonel Gunther, the technician worked for the KGB.

"Who else heard this?" General Mendez tapped the roll of reel-to-reel magnetic tape.

"No one, General. I dismissed all the other technicians from the project. When I heard the interrogation, I... realized the significance immediately."

"Good. Return to the communications suite. Wait for my instructions. We may need to communicate with our friends."

General Mendez meant their friends at the Soviet Embassy.

"Yes, my commander." Saluting, the technician left the office.

The telephone buzzed. A static-scratched voice came through the receiver as one of the field units reported via the highest-priority channel, a secure-frequency radio-telephone channel that linked the unit leaders directly to their commander.

"The Ochoas captured one of the gringos," a unit officer reported.

"What of Colonel Gunther?"

"Nothing yet."

"And the others?"

"They are with the army."

"Does an officer loyal to the International command that army detail?"

"Yes. But he says he must wait to take the Americans. The time is not right for his move."

"Tell them to bring the captured American to the underground garage at this address." The general told the technician the name and number of an office building only a hundred meters away from the Trans-Americas tower.

"They want the reward, General. They say they will not deliver him until they see the money."

"Then have the Ochoas bring him. Our units will escort the Ochoas. Then they will receive their reward. Order ten men to take positions around the garage. They must be concealed and waiting when the Ochoas come."

"That is very close to these offices. Could that compromise our operations here?"

"I will supervise the. . .the payoff. I do not have time to travel across the city."

The general hung up the phone. He could not risk an interrogation of the American. He could not risk anything the American might have already told the Ochoas. The American and all the Ochoas who captured him must be annihilated.

When they came to deliver the prisoner, all would receive the same reward.

Death.

"Amigo, I will explain."

Lyons lay on the concrete floor, his ankles tied, his hands bound behind him. Coral stood over him while other Ochoa gunmen searched Lyons for weapons. They found revolvers, the reengineered Colt Government Model, the Uzi, a knife and the Atchisson. The collection of weapons went into a burlap bag. The hand-radio went to Coral, who slipped it into his coat pocket.

"What is there to explain? How much Gunther promised to pay you?"

"I will explain how valuable you are to the International."

Lyons spun on his hip and kicked Coral with both feet. The Mexican staggered back. The other Ochoa men grabbed Lyons, immobilizing him on the floor.

"You are a fighter," Coral said, laughing. He limped back to Lyons. "The International hired many gunmen today. We joined them also. There is a reward for any of you Americans—one hundred thousand American dollars. Very good, yes? Now we take you to them."

The gunmen of the Ochoa gang carried Lyons to a panel truck. They threw him inside. Lyons thrashed and struggled, straining against the ropes that dug into his wrists. But the men sat across his legs and back.

A Mexican army colonel in uniform leaned into the truck. Behind him, Lyons saw soldiers in camou fatigues. The colonel grabbed Lyons by his hair and jerked his head back. Lyons twisted his head, tried to throw off the weight of the men on his back, and the colonel laughed at him.

Steel clanked. The warehouse doors opened. The

colonel and his soldiers stepped back as Coral slammed the truck's cargo doors closed. Then they drove from the garage. The truck sped through crowds of curious people, its horn sounding.

"You believe I betrayed you, yes?" Coral asked Lyons.

"You Nazi scumbag," spat Lyons. "All your talk about understanding Mexico, about poverty, about troubles."

Coral laughed. "You do believe! Let us hope the colonel also believes I betrayed you, too. But it is not true."

"Then what is?"

"I took Gunther to my friends. We wanted information from him. We want revenge against the Blancos and Gunther knows who they are. But he told us nothing. He can tell us nothing—"

"You killed him?"

"No, it is that drug. When he is awake, he makes noises and sees things. Sometimes he sleeps. Until the drug is over, he is like an idiot. You will see. He will join us in a few minutes."

"And why do you do this?" Lyons demanded, arching his back to motion with his tied hands.

Coral smiled. "Because you, you we will take to the International. You and Gunther." Coral motioned to the men sitting on Lyons. He felt hands grip his wrists, then a knife cut the ropes on his hands and feet. Another man passed him the burlap bag containing his weapons.

Glancing through the windshield, Lyons saw unmarked police cars leading the panel truck through traffic. Other cars followed.

"Now do you understand? How else could we go directly to the headquarters of the International?"

"What about my partners?"

Coral passed the hand-radio to Lyons. "Inform them."

"What about the lieutenant and the sergeant? Are they with the International?"

"I do not know. You see, we told the fascists that we work for them. We told them to find you, to follow you. The truck that followed you this morning, from the old garage? One of our people. But you lost him in traffic. We searched everywhere in the city. One of our people told us of the soldiers and North Americans renting a warehouse. We had our men around the warehouse. We wanted to talk, so you did not think we betrayed you, but the army comes and then the Blancos come and the shooting starts. We watched the fight from the roof. The lieutenant and his men fought the fascists. They are honest. I don't know about the sergeant."

Lyons keyed his hand-radio. He clicked only the transmit. One click to identify himself, three clicks as a coded "no." He repeated the one click, then three clicks, hoping Gadgets and Blancanales would understand.

Three clicks followed by three more clicks answered. Three clicks meant Gadgets. Then Gadgets repeated the code. Lyons waited. Gadgets would need time to walk away from the others so he could speak.

A flurry of clicks came. Voices and sounds came from the hand-radio. Lyons heard fists striking flesh. Then a voice came on.

"Okay, what is it?"

But the voice had a Spanish accent. Again the voice spoke, trying to get Lyons to answer.

"Okay, tell me what...."

The International had taken his partners.

15

In the underground garage, General Mendez positioned his men in a line behind concrete pillars and
parked cars. Each gunman carried an FN FAL rifle.
When the Ochoas descended the ramp from the
avenida, they would drive directly into the ambush.
The thin sheet metal of the Ochoa truck would not
even slow the 7.62 NATO slugs fired by the FN FAL
rifles.

An officer ran to the general. "Commander, urgent messages!"

"What?"

"Colonel Larde has the two other Americans. The
Mexicans escaped, but he brings the gringos."

"Good. What is the other?"

"A problem, commander. The captain of the
squads escorting the Ochoas waits to speak with
you."

The general went to the four-door Dodge containing his secure-frequency radio. He took the microphone. "This is your commander."

"The Ochoas have Colonel Gunther."

"Where is he? Send him to me immediately. Is he
wounded?"

"He is in the truck of the Ochoas. The truck that
carries the American prisoner."

"What! Why did you allow that?"

"It happened too quickly, General. They stopped. Men transferred the colonel from a car to the truck. Then the truck started again."

"Are you sure it was Colonel Gunther?"

"We saw him in the lights of cars. I know the colonel. I am sure it was him."

"This changes everything. Radio the other cars! When the Ochoas' truck enters the garage, all your cars will follow. Do you understand? No one fires until we free Colonel Gunther. No one fires until he is clear."

"I understand," the unit leader answered. "I will brief all the others."

General Mendez switched off the transmitter and rushed to the waiting gunmen. He had to cancel the ambush.

As THE PANEL TRUCK SPED through the evening traffic, escorted by the unmarked police cars, Lyons and the Ochoa gunmen prepared for the surprise attack on the International. Lyons pushed aside the unconscious Gunther to clear a space on the panel truck's floor. Then he field-checked his weapons, beginning with the silenced Colt Government Model. He worked the action and tested the seating of the suppressor. He loaded a 10-round extended magazine. An Ochoa gunman gave him a handful of .45-caliber hardball cartridges to reload his spare magazines. Those mags went into Lyons's left-hand coat pocket.

Then he checked his backup Python.

The Ochoas also provided 12-gauge double-ought cartridges to top off his Atchisson mag.

The Ochoas carried an assortment of weapons. Coral, the oldest and most heavily armed, had two revolvers, one in a shoulder holster, another in an ankle rig. He had a pistol-grip double-barreled shotgun sawed off to six inches that went into a coat pocket. And he carried an old Thompson .45 with two 30-round magazines taped end to end.

Knowing what they would face when they attacked the International, the other three gunmen carried high-cyclic-rate assault weapons. One man had a standard Uzi and a Mini-Uzi. Another man had a .45-caliber Ingram. The third man carried an Uzi and a pistol-grip Remington 1100. And all the Ochoa men wore bulletproof vests.

On the wide Paseo de la Reforma, only seconds away from the meeting with the commander of the International, Coral turned to Lyons. "We must make you our prisoner again. That shotgun, that Uzi—" he pointed to the two weapons in Lyons's hands "—have them near, but—"

"Yeah, yeah. I understand." Lyons found the ropes that had bound his wrists. He put his hands behind his back and one of the Ochoa men wrapped the rope around his wrists. Lyons held both ends of the unknotted rope in his fists. Another length of rope went around his ankles. The gunman tied the rope with a slipknot, then tucked the slipknot into Lyons's sock.

"Be ready," Coral told his men.

The line of escort cars slowed. Weaving through traffic, an unmarked police car sped ahead. Coral looked out to see the car pass. For an instant, he saw into its interior. Then the car swerved in front of the first unmarked police car and raced down the ramp into the underground garage.

"That was the others!" Coral told Lyons. "Your Americans. I saw them in the back."

"If we can free them, that'll be seven of us. Wish we could have brought the Yaquis. But in a way, I'm glad we couldn't."

"They will be here soon. Many others will come."

"Good." Lyons looked over to the unconscious Gunther. "As soon as we're moving, we have to get him someplace safe. We've brought him too far to lose him now to stray bullets."

On the floor, his hands tied behind him, his feet tied, Gunther eased one eye open to a slit. He did not move or otherwise betray himself. His eye glanced to the men around him. Then his eyelid closed. He waited.

The caravan descended into the underground garage.

"What do you see?" Lyons asked, flat on the floor.

"There are many men around. They take the North Americans out of the car. A Mexican colonel goes to an old man in a suit. The colonel salutes the old man. Maybe the old one is General Mendez."

"What about my partners?"

"The soldiers and *pistoleros* punch them. But they stop. Now we arrive. Be ready."

Lyons heard voices outside. The truck's doors opened, then the cargo doors opened. Coral dragged out Lyons and dropped him on the concrete.

As the gunmen of the International kicked him, Lyons saw Gadgets and Blancanales only a step away.

"Where's the general?" Coral called out. "I want my gold!"

Gunther bellowed, "Shoot them! It's a trick!"

A gray-haired man in a gray business suit stood several steps away. "Give them their reward!" he commanded with a sneer across his patrician features.

Hands went under sports jackets as the gunmen of the International reached for their holstered pistols.

"Pol! Wizard! Down!" Lyons yelled. "Get down! Down!" Without taking the second to untie his feet, Lyons shouldered and twisted his way through the legs of the fascists. A fascist kicked him in the face twice, but Lyons turned away and crawled on. He grabbed the ankles of his partners and dragged them down.

As the Americans went flat, the four Ochoas scythed down the gunmen of the International.

Coral aimed the six-inch-long sawed-off shotgun at General Mendez. Two fascists stepped in the way of the blast. The brains of the first man sprayed over the man behind him. As the headless body dropped, a second blast from the shotgun sheared away the face of the other man and punched holes in a third soldier's neck. Only two of the double-ought lead balls hit the general.

One of the general's arms jerked back as a .33-caliber ball broke the bone. The second ball hit just above his belt, a spot of red appearing on his white silk shirt.

The general staggered back, whining with pain as the scene exploded in front of him. Coral pocketed his shotgun pistol and shouldered his Thompson.

On both sides of Coral, his men emptied their submachine guns, firing without aiming, simply holding their weapons at stomach height and firing from one side of the crowd to the other. High-velocity 9mm hardball bullets punched through fascists to kill again. The .45 slugs in Coral's Thompson and his friend's Ingram ripped through men, throwing their bodies back.

Blood and casings fell on Able Team. The autofire from the Ochoas seemed to be one continuous explosion, the noise and the blast continuing for seconds as the four Ochoa *pistoleros* killed or maimed every standing man.

As corpses dropped around him, Lyons pulled the knife from his pocket and cut the ropes tying the hands of his partners. Then he freed his feet with one quick cut.

"The Man of Iron does it again!" Gadgets yelled, grabbing an Uzi from the tangle of dead men on the floor around them.

"Is that Miguel Coral?" Blancanales asked.

"Whose side is he on now?" Gadgets demanded.

"Our side. The escape was a trick on the Nazis," Lyons said as he unholstered the Python. He covered his partners, giving them time to find weapons.

The parked cars shielded Able Team. In the kill-zone, only the panicked and the dead and the screaming wounded remained. The other fascist squads, beyond the cars, did not have a direct line of fire at Able Team lying flat on the concrete.

A fascist running for cover turned, Uzi in hand. Lyons snap-fired, the X-head hollowpoint hitting the Uzi's handle, the gunman's right hand exploding as the 158-grain high-velocity slug shattered on the steel of the weapon. The tangled ruins of the gunman's hand flopped at the end of his arm as he staggered backward into a car. Nine-millimeter slugs from behind Lyons punched into the wounded man's chest.

A fascist ran from behind the shelter of a concrete pillar with an FN FAL para-rifle. Lyons steadied his Python in both hands. Before the para-rifle reached the fascist's shoulder, a .357 slug smashed through his forehead.

Shotgun blasts went off above them. Wadding and hot powder rained on them. Lyons grabbed an Uzi from the hands of a corpse. Flat on the concrete, he emptied the Uzi in a wild, one-handed spray in the direction of the fascist gunmen. Then he dropped the empty weapon and crawled through blood to the panel truck.

Heavy-caliber slugs punched through the truck, glass flying. Lyons looked inside.

No Gunther.

Lyons grabbed his Atchisson and the Uzi he had captured in the alley firefight. He saw Coral and the others firing from the cover of a bullet-pocked Dodge a few steps away.

Blancanales and Gadgets crawled through the slaughter. They both had Uzis over their shoulders. Magazines weighed down their pockets. Each held an autopistol in one hand.

"Move it, Ironman!" Gadgets shouted as they ran to join Coral.

Blood puddled on the oily concrete. Staying low, Lyons looked for Gunther in the tangle of corpses. He saw a headless corpse and a man with his hands knotted in his spilled intestines, and a wounded man vomiting blood. One fascist crawled away, dragging a shattered leg. A shotgun blast struck him low in the back, his clothing suddenly torn and bloody as his broken-backed corpse flopped.

But no Gunther.

Lyons crabbed under the panel truck, then scrambled for the wall of parked cars, calling out, *"¡Amigos! ¡Mis amigos Ochoas! ¡No dispare!"*

An Ochoa man reloading a Remington 1100 gave him a salute and a grin. To the side, a revolver popped and a light went out. Gadgets sat against the shelter of a police car, plinking at the overhead lights with a captured .38 revolver. One by one, he shot out the light bulbs.

"Where's Gunther?" Lyons yelled out. *"¿Dónde está Gunther?"*

"No se," answered the Ochoa with the Remington.

"It happened too fast," Coral shouted. "But he is here. We will find him. He will not escape you."

Gadgets popped out another light. "That ain't the question. Our problem at the moment is for us to escape them."

"Wrong attitude, Wizard." Lyons flicked the safety off his Atchisson. Heavy with weapons and ammunition—the assault shotgun in his hands, an Uzi over his shoulder, pistols in his holsters and pockets, magazines in other pockets—he moved to the side.

Blancanales followed him. The Ochoa with the Remington joined the North Americans as they slipped from parked car to parked car. Gadgets fired above them, still popping light bulbs.

Gunmen of the International spotted Lyons's flanking team. Heavy-caliber slugs punched the cars. Other fascists sprayed 9mm autofire at the concrete, trying to create skipping ricochets under the cars to wound the flankers.

Flat on his belly as NATO-caliber slugs came through the car door above him, Lyons saw feet running. He fired under the car, the double-ought buckshot bouncing off the concrete. A foot disappeared. The gunman staggered forward, trying to run on the bones of his ankle but falling. Lyons fired again, at a distance of ten feet, the load of buckshot tearing a two-inch-wide hole through the fascist's torso.

The dead man had an FN FAL para-rifle. He wore a bandolier of magazines. Keeping his head down, Lyons stripped the man of his weapons and ammunition. He also found a 9mm autopistol. He passed the FN FAL to Blancanales.

Continuing in a semicircle, they came to a traffic lane. Lyons looked out from behind a parked car. Fascists fired an explosion of 9mm slugs at him. Bullets popped the tire near his ear.

"Pol! I'm going across. You and Señor Remington put out some fire. On three. One! Two! Three!"

Weapons fired in one long blast. Lyons dived across the traffic lane to the shelter of a concrete pillar. As he scrambled behind the pillar, bullets chipped the other side, ricochets whining to hit concrete and cars.

Lyons crabbed another few feet to a parked truck. He saw polished shoes and pressed slacks. A gunman pointed his Uzi down at Lyons and Lyons rolled and fired the Atchisson one-handed, the blast catching the fascist in the crotch, flipping the man face first onto the concrete. His arteries pumping jets of blood out of a vast wound, the fascist tried to raise himself on his arms.

Lyons did not waste another 12-gauge round. Standing, he brought the butt of the Atchisson down on the back of the man's neck, snapping his vertebrae.

Another gunman ran around the back of the truck. Point-blank, Lyons put a 12-gauge blast through the man's face.

"Pol!"

"Can't! Cannot do it."

Letting his assault shotgun hang from his shoulder by its sling, Lyons snatched up the Uzis of the dead men. An Uzi in his left hand, he leaned from cover and sprayed out the magazine. Return fire smashed into the truck. Lyons felt blood flowing down his arm. Blood dripped from his sleeve.

The blood of other men covered his sports coat. He could not see his own wound. He could not stop to find it. Dropping the blood-slick Uzi, he shifted his position. NATO slugs tore through the truck as riflemen tried to kill him.

Blancanales answered with the FN FAL para-rifle.

Over the sights of the Uzi, Lyons saw a fascist stagger back. Then the Remington 1100 blasted a gunman's face and hands away. Lyons spotted a leg and put a burst of 9mm slugs through it. As the wounded man clawed at the concrete, another burst killed him.

Fascists retreated to the ramp, trying to gain the safety of the street. The Ochoas cut them down with shotguns and bursts of .45-caliber slugs. Gadgets broke cover and pursued the fascists, firing quick bursts from an Uzi into any fascist still holding a weapon.

A wounded man with a pistol got a 3-shot burst to the face. A running fascist got four 9mm slugs through the back. A soldier in camouflage-patterned fatigues tried to tear a grenade from his web belt but died.

Lyons changed magazines and charged, killing everyone in front of him. Wounded men, fascists crawling to escape—blasts of 12-gauge ended their allegiance to the Pan-American Reich.

A shot zipped past Lyons's face. He whirled, unleashing a full-auto burst from his Atchisson. A fascist with a pistol disintegrated as three blasts of double-ought and number-two buckshot ripped away an arm, opened his chest and tore off his head.

"Where's General Mendez? Where's Gunther?" Lyons shouted to the others as he searched for another Atchisson magazine in his pockets.

"I think the general made it out," Gadgets called back. As the firing died, he took that moment to change Uzi mags. "I haven't seen Gunther."

A full-auto burst from an M-16 chipped concrete, the high-velocity 5.56mm slugs whining and ricocheting through the garage.

Caught in the open with empty weapons, Lyons and Gadgets looked up the ramp. Lieutenant Soto and a wall of black-clad Mexican army commandos stood at the top.

Each of their rifles pointed at the North Americans.

16

Spinning to face the line of soldiers, Lyons slammed a magazine into his assault shotgun and thumbed down the fire-selector to full auto.

Gadgets screamed, *"Don't. They're good guys!"*

Lyons stopped an instant before his index finger touched the trigger. "What?"

"Yeah, man. The lieutenant's okay. He tried to stop the colonel from taking us here. And he got banged upside the head for thanks."

Setting the safety of his Atchisson, Lyons strode up the ramp to the Mexican soldiers. The lieutenant directed his soldiers to form a cordon around the entrance. He motioned Lyons back.

"You cannot be seen," Lieutenant Soto told him. The young officer accompanied him down the ramp. Lyons saw that a huge scab of drying blood matted the lieutenant's black hair. "There will be much trouble soon. I may lose my commission. Or I may be a hero. But first we must do what must be done."

"Now do you know what's going on?" Lyons asked.

"Yes, now I know."

Blancanales greeted the lieutenant with a quick medical exam. "How's your head? Do you feel dizzy? Nauseated? Do you have a medic with you?"

"We cannot take the time," the lieutenant replied. "The criminals fled to another building. When we attempted to detain the fascists, they fired on my men. We know where they are, but an assault from the street is not possible. What do you know of these fascists?"

Blancanales saw blood dripping from Lyons's coat sleeve. "You got hit."

"Their commander is someone named General Mendez," Lyons answered the lieutenant first. Then he made a fist and moved his arm for Blancanales to see. "It still works."

"Alfonso Deloria Mendez was very important in the previous administration," the lieutenant told them. "I recognized him from parades. That means we must act tonight. Now, he probably calls the ex-president and his friends for help. Tomorrow we cannot touch him."

As the lieutenant spoke, Miguel Coral joined the group. Lyons turned to him. "They ran to a building near here," he said to Coral. "You know anything about it?"

"Nothing. What is the problem?"

"They look down on the *avenida*," Lieutenant Soto said. "Their machine guns fired down on my men. We cannot assault from the street. And we cannot call for other units. No airborne troops, no armored forces. I only trust the men with me. And you North Americans."

"No other way into the building?" Blancanales asked. "Is it possible we could fire down from another building?"

"The tower of Trans-Americas S.A. is the highest in the area."

Coral glanced at his watch. "Soon, with luck, you will have your airborne forces. Perhaps *ahorita*."

"What?" the lieutenant asked.

"The helicopter. When our surveillance men saw you soldiers, we warned the pilot, Señor Davis, and the Yaqui. They went to get the helicopter. We thought it would be the best way to escape the city."

"And what about Vato and Ixto?" Lyons asked.

"I will radio." Coral called to one of his men. The man took a walkie-talkie from the panel truck and ran to Coral. Flipping the switch, they heard only static. Coral went up the ramp to the open air. He spoke into the radio. After a few seconds, he returned.

"The helicopter comes. All the boys are with it."

"We will take the helicopter," the lieutenant told the North Americans. "With it, my platoons can land on the top of the building, where the criminals will not expect them."

Gadgets glanced to the blood-splashed, corpse-littered floor of the garage. "The unexpected is hitting a lot of people today," he said.

"THOUGHT YOU DIDN'T WANT TO FLY this thing anymore." Leaning forward to the pilot station, Lyons shouted over the rotor noise to Davis. The DEA pilot checked his instruments as soldiers boarded the helicopter.

"I don't! This thing's junk." Davis turned to glance at the soldiers crowding through the door. He saw Lyons's clothes. "Man, you look like you been rolling in blood."

"I have."

"I believe it. Your gear's back there. All those Mexicans are in blacksuits. And from what I understand, they're going to be shooting goons who are wearing clothes just like those. There could be a misunderstanding."

"You talked me into it," Lyons said, glancing back to check out the packs of gear secured to the seat frames and the gun mount.

The helicopter idled on the roof of a high rise. A block away, the Trans-Americas S.A. tower stood against the sky, its office lights creating random patterns of white and black. Several soldiers stood outside the radius of the rotor blades. They would take the next flight to the roof of the fascist headquarters.

Lyons tossed out his partners' gear. "Wizard! Pol!"

"Thanks," Gadgets shouted. "You go with the lieutenant. We'll come over on the second trip." Gadgets carried the packs back to Blancanales, waiting with the Yaquis.

Lyons's pack had been lashed to the door gun's mount by its hip belt. He pushed aside the barrel of the M-60 and stripped off his blood-crusted sports coat and shirt. He paused to find the wound. A bullet had grazed his left forearm. It would not even need stitches. Just another scar.

He did not take the time to change from his gray slacks. He pulled on his faded black fatigue shirt. It stank of sweat and dust from the Sonora desert. Over his fatigue shirt, he slipped on his Kevlar and steel battle armor and slapped the Velcro closures. The Kevlar would stop all low-velocity bullets and shrapnel. The steel trauma-plate insert over his heart and lungs would stop all rifle bullets. The armor had saved his life before, stopping a point-blank burst from a Kalashnikov in an Able Team battle in Cairo.

A second later, the helicopter lifted away. Lyons buckled bandoliers of ammunition and grenades over the black battle armor. He transferred his Colt from the shoulder holster to his web belt's holster. He touched the Python in the hideaway holster at the small of his back. Two speedloaders went into his pants' pocket. Then he fastened the safety strap around his waist and leaned out the side door.

The helicopter flew over canyons of light. Lines of headlights and taillights marked the *avenida*. Vertical walls of glass shimmered with reflections of the traffic lights and neon. Electric billboards flashed with colored lights.

Even at hundreds of meters above the streets, the night smelled of auto pollution.

Rising above the other corporate buildings, the tower of Trans-Americas S.A. had a penthouse topped with satellite dishes and radio antennae. The circle and crossed lines of a helipad marked an open area of asphalt. Lights illuminated the helipad. A wind sock hung on a pole, motionless in the gray night.

Lyons saw figures leaving the penthouse. Two gunmen carried a stretcher. Other gunmen saw the helicopter and waved.

The lieutenant pointed and shouted. "Perhaps that is General Mendez they carry. I think they wait for an army helicopter. Understand why I would not call for help?"

"*Entiendo.*" Lyons nodded. He spoke into the intercom. "Fly-boy, take us in straight. Time for another surprise."

"You specialists are very surprising fellows."

"Keeps us alive."

"Until someone surprises you."

"Never happen. We're ready for anything. Boy Scout motto...."

On the helipad, a gunman pointed at the approaching troopship. Another gunman raised an Uzi. The crowd of fascists unslung weapons. Davis banked the helicopter away and shouted through the headphones. "You ready for a hot LZ?"

Slugs clanked into the fuselage. The helicopter veered away. Lyons looked down at the lights of the *avenida,* then the helicopter returned to level flight.

As the Mexicans raked the rooftop with their M-16 rifles, Lyons slung his Atchisson over his shoulder. Trusting his life to the safety webbing, he stood behind the pedestal-mounted M-60. He pulled the belt of 7.62 NATO cartridges from the can. Locking back the bolt, he set the safety and opened the feed-tray cover and positioned the first cartridge in the feed-tray groove. He closed the cover and eased forward the bolt to chamber the first round. He sighted on the stretcher.

If he killed General Mendez, he killed the commander of the International in Mexico.

Green tracers from the M-60 skipped off the asphalt helipad and pinwheeled into the night. A fascist gunman staggered back and fell over the stretcher. Other gunmen threw the dead man aside. They grabbed the handles of the stretcher and ran for shelter. Lyons held the sights on the white-wrapped man on the stretcher. One of the gunmen carrying the stretcher fell.

The helicopter gained altitude, throwing Lyons's line of fire off. He saw the surviving gunman drag the stretcher into the penthouse. Lyons spoke into the intercom. "Davis, circle level and hold it."

As the helicopter dropped, Lyons saw muzzle-flashes in the windows of the penthouse. He sighted on the dark windows and fired, holding the trigger back as the line of green tracers shattered the windows and punched through the walls. He saw green zigzags inside the penthouse as tracers ricocheted through the interior.

Grazing fire from a machine gun and the M-16 rifles of the Mexican soldiers drove the fascists off the rooftop. Lyons spoke into the intercom again. "Put us down."

The helicopter rose higher. Lyons leaned out the door and fired straight down into the roof of the penthouse, punching 7.62mm holes through microwave antennae and electronic components. A relay box exploded in a spray of sparks. Lyons continued firing—through the roof, through the walls, then directly through the door and windows—until the helicopter descended and the skids hit the helipad.

Soldiers rushed past Lyons. A submachine gun flashed from the penthouse. A soldier fell. As the wounded man crawled to cover, the other soldiers went flat, directing fire at the gunman while another soldier ran to the right. On the run, he pulled a grenade from his web belt and tossed it through the window.

Designed to stun terrorists and hostages with a blinding white flash and overwhelming shock without the wounds of shrapnel, the antiterrorist grenade exploded and blew glass and debris from the penthouse. The soldier threw a second grenade inside.

The platoon rushed the ruined penthouse. No more firing came from inside.

Sprawled on the asphalt, a wounded gunman raised himself from his blood and fired an Uzi. Shot in the legs, a soldier dropped. The gunman continued firing at the wounded soldier, a bullet knocking his M-16 from his hands. Lyons fired a single blast of 12-gauge, the double-ought load, taking away the fascist's head.

As a medic tended the wounded soldiers, Lyons followed the Mexican commandos into the wreckage of the penthouse.

Flashlights revealed dead men, groaning wounded, smashed furniture. Overturned file cabinets spilled thousands of papers. Blood puddled on the Persian carpets.

Soldiers searched through the destroyed office, shining flashlights on the faces of the dead and wounded. They did not find General Mendez or Colonel Gunther.

A private elevator connected the penthouse to the lower floors. The lieutenant posted four men to watch the elevator and the wounded fascists. Then he led his men out to the roof again.

Far below, they heard shooting. The lieutenant's walkie-talkie buzzed. He spoke into the radio for a moment. Then he directed his men to search the roof.

"They attempted to escape through the garage," Lieutenant Soto told Lyons. "My sergeant's platoon turned them back. They are trapped now."

A soldier shouted. He pointed to a door.

"Those are the stairs down," the lieutenant told Lyons. "Are you ready?"

"Consider this, Lieutenant," Lyons replied. "These Nazis are murderers. They're involved in the drug syndicates. Many of them are foreigners who are wanted for atrocities in their own countries. If they surrender, it's execution or life in prison. Chances are, they'll fight to the death."

"What do you suggest?"

"Withdraw your soldiers. Send word that the ex-president has arranged an escape for the Nazis. Then send helicopters to take them away. And take them directly to prison. Otherwise, you'll lose half your men in the building. Too many young men will die for other people's politics."

Lieutenant Soto clasped Lyons's shoulder in his hand. "American, you're a good man. But if I am to rid my country—if we are to rid our countries of these fascists, it must be tonight. Now. Tomorrow we may be in prison. You understand? I have no other way. We are alone in this."

Lyons nodded. *"Entiendo."*

The helicopter returned. As it touched down on the helipad, soldiers jumped from the doors. Gadgets and Blancanales jogged over to Lyons. They wore their battle armor and gear.

Lyons touch-checked his weapons. "Hold off on the assault until me and my partners are ready."

"We must start now," the lieutenant said.

"We only need a heavy rope. And then we will lead the assault."

"No, you are foreigners," argued the lieutenant. "This is my duty."

"Let foreigners fight foreigners," Lyons insisted.

17

Shock-flash grenades boomed. As the Mexican soldiers sprayed autofire down the stairwells, Lyons dropped off the edge of the roof.

Thirty floors above the Paseo de la Reforma, he hung on the end of a rope. The overhang of the roof placed him six feet from the windows. He watched the offices in front of him. Three windows down, men moved inside an executive suite. But the explosions and shooting in the stairwells kept the attention of the fascists away from the skyline of Mexico City.

Lyons looked down. The lights of police cars and ambulances surrounded the tower. Emergency barriers blocked the *avenida*. He saw the specks of police officers and soldiers, but no one immediately below him.

He waited until his side-to-side swinging stopped. Then he moved back and forth to swing toward the plate-glass windows. He built up his swing. His shoes touched the steel frame. He pushed off.

With his silenced Colt, he fired four slugs through the plate glass as he swung outward, one shot to each corner. The glass shattered in sheets. Most of the glass fell into the office, but some fell to the empty sidewalk.

As he swung in, he reached out an arm to put it

through the empty window frame and grab a hand-hold on the inside.

Slowly he eased through the window. Nothing moved in the dark office. He untied the harness of rope around him. Then he went to the door and locked it. By the light from the gray sky, he searched the office. He found only desks and filing cabinets.

He paused to reload his Colt, slapping in another extended 10-round-capacity magazine.

Returning to the window, he knocked out the last pieces of plate glass in the frame. He gave the rope two jerks, then two more. After a few seconds, the rope went slack. He pulled the lower end of the rope into the office and tied it to a heavy desk.

He jerked the rope three times. Above him on the roof, his partners pulled in the slack. The rope now stretched taut from the top of the window to the desk. Lyons grabbed the rope, twisting it and jumping on it to try the knots.

A moment later, Gadgets slid through the window. Lyons cut the rope harness from his partner and freed him from the safety rope. If the taut line had failed as Gadgets slid down, the safety would have stopped his fall. They threw the safety rope back through the window. On the roof, Blancanales and the Mexican commandos pulled it up.

"Anything?" Gadgets whispered.

"Nothing yet. Heard voices. But I know they didn't hear me."

"Positive?"

"No one's shooting at us."

Blancanales slid down next. They cut away his harness, then sent the safety rope up again. They unslung their weapons and listened to the firing coming from the stairwells. The booms of shock-flash grenades punctuated the firefight of the sham attack. Able Team each carried four of the antiterrorist stun grenades. As they waited, they jammed valved hearing protectors in their ears.

A Mexican commando came down. Able Team left him to supervise the entry of the other soldiers. Lyons went first with his silenced Colt. Gadgets stood behind him with a shock-flash ready.

Easing the office door open, Lyons saw men in uniforms and street clothes rushing through the corridor. Some of the gunmen wore the gray uniform of the International, others the OD fatigues of the Mexican army. He saw traffic cops in their dark pants and sky-blue shirts. But most of the gunmen wore the uniform he had seen in actions in San Francisco, Los Angeles and Guatemala City: expensive European casual suits, tailored and pressed.

But the airborne assault had ruined the styling of the International soldiers. Blood from superficial wounds stained their Italian fashions. They had torn their slacks and sports coats, wrinkled their silk shirts, scuffed their shoes.

Lyons turned to Gadgets and whispered, "Fragmentation."

Gadgets returned the shock-flash grenade to his combat harness. Lyons unhooked two Italian MU-50G controlled-effect grenades from his gear. He pointed to the right and held up the two small grenades. He pointed to the left and held up two fingers. Gadgets nodded and took two MU-50G grenades from his bandolier. They nodded to each other and pulled the safety pins.

"One...two..." Lyons counted, "three!"

They threw the grenades in opposite directions and slammed the door shut. Gadgets laughed. "Designer grenades for designer dudes!"

The chain-blast came an instant later. Lyons charged out first, Atchisson leveled, Gadgets one step behind him. Blancanales and a Mexican commando cut to the right.

Only emergency lamps provided light. The storm of high-velocity steel beads had broken all the fluorescent tubes. Lyons and Gadgets rushed over the dead and wounded. Pointing his CAR with one hand, Gadgets fired 5.56mm execution shots into any gunman who still lived. Lyons did not waste his 12-gauge shells.

At the door to the executive suite, Lyons fired a single blast through the lock and the door flew open. Submachine guns fired, slugs splintering the door, punching through the thin office walls. Gadgets dropped flat on the carpet and tossed in a shock-flash.

The white blast silenced the weapons. Dashing into the twilight of the office, they saw men and women sprawled around computer terminals. Shattered video displays smoked with phosphor powder. Flashlight in his left hand, the Atchisson's pistol-grip in his right, Lyons checked the stunned fascists while Gadgets watched the door.

He counted five men and three women. But no General Mendez. No Colonel Gunther.

"Call for some soldiers," Lyons told his partner as they went to the office door. "We can't stop to tie these Nazis up."

"*¡Gringo putos!*"

A woman shot Lyons in the back.

Lyons spun and the woman fired her revolver again, a .38-caliber slug roaring past his ear. One blast from the Atchisson tore apart her heart and lungs, throwing her body over. Dying, she tried to scream, her eyes fluttering, her hands opening and closing reflexively as liters of her blood drained from the vast through-and-through wound.

Gadgets picked the deformed hollowpoint out of Lyons's Kevlar and gave it to him. "Teach you to turn your back on a woman."

Plaster flew from the walls. Gadgets staggered, and Lyons felt a slash across his gut and right forearm. An autoweapon in the corridor fired burst after burst at the doorway. As Lyons went down backward, his arm screaming with pain, he brought up the Atchisson.

An International gunman, ammunition bandoliers belted across his sports coat, ran through the door. He fired an M-16 wildly, spraying the office at waist height. Squinting against the muzzle-flash above him, Lyons snap-fired a single blast.

Steel shot smashed the plastic-and-aluminum autorifle to scrap, tearing away the gunman's hand, ripping through his chest. He fell back into another fascist attacker. Lyons aimed the Atchisson and fired again, slamming the dead men back some more. The corpses fell in the corridor.

Autofire searched for Lyons, hammering the door,

shattering plastic computer components on the desk tops. Gadgets groaned, then rolled across the floor to the doorway. He found a fragmentation grenade in his web gear. Pulling the pin, he let the safety lever flip off. He counted away the delay.

A fascist dashed across the doorway, an autorifle in his hands flashing. Roaring over Gadgets's head, the slugs swept the office. Gadgets tossed the grenade into the corridor and scrambled back as slugs whined off the doorframe. Burst after burst killed the carpet where he had sprawled only a second before.

The grenade stopped the firing. Blinded, a hundred wounds spurting blood, the gunman staggered to the office door. He held the wall and screamed with shock and despair. Lyons pointed his Atchisson at the dying fascist but did not fire. He crawled to help Gadgets as the screaming man died on his feet and fell.

"I'm hit...."

"Where?" His Atchisson pointed at the door, Lyons searched for blood on Gadgets with his left hand.

"There!" Gadgets gasped as Lyons touched the Kevlar over the left side of his chest.

Blood oozed through a tear in the battle armor. Though the steel trauma plate set in his armor protected him from a straight-on shot to his chest, a 5.56mm bullet had hit Gadgets from the side. Kevlar could not stop full-velocity rifle bullets. Lyons fumbled with the Velcro closure strips.

"Hey, let me take care of me." Gadgets pulled open his battle armor. "And you take care of you. Now your other arm's bleeding."

Checking himself, Lyons saw where a bullet had slashed across his battle armor, cutting a path across the black nylon exterior. The bullet had continued into his right arm. He pushed the sleeve up, saw two bloody holes where the bullet had entered and exited just below the inside of his elbow. Pain came when he made a fist, but his hand still functioned. The shallow wound had not severed any tendons.

"No doubt about it," Gadgets said, trying to twist his face into a grin. He pointed to a small hole in his ribs. "I'm shot."

Black uniformed commandos ran into the suite. For an instant, Lyons and Gadgets looked into the bores of the Mexicans' M-16 rifles, then a commando went to one knee beside the North Americans.

The Mexican tore open a field-dressing packet and pressed a bandage to the wound. Gadgets pushed the dressing aside. He probed at the wound with his fingers.

Blancanales joined them. "You hit? Where?"

"I'll live. I'm okay, I think. Nothing broken. Not gargling blood. Ughh—there it is. Found it. The wall and the Kevlar almost stopped it."

"Stay here," Lyons told him. "Pol, let's go."

As Gadgets surrendered to the first aid, Blancanales stripped off his partner's ammunition and grenades. Gadgets tried to sit up.

Lyons pushed him back. "Take a break. I'll call you if we need you."

"Get the number-one man!"

"That's the plan...."

Lyons and Blancanales rushed into the corridor.

Two Mexican commandos followed the North Americans. Firing continued at the stairwells. Bypassing the offices, the group went to the next corridor. Lyons dropped flat and looked around the corner.

In one instant of sight, as boots ran toward him, Lyons saw the elevator lobby. A group of International soldiers in uniforms and casual styles defended the stairs, spraying autofire up at the attacking Mexican commandos, then closing the door as the Mexicans returned the fire. Across the lobby, other gunmen shoved personnel—men, women, wounded—into the elevators.

Then a boot kicked Lyons as a soldier tripped over him. Blancanales brought down the butt of his M-16/M-203 on the back of the fascist soldier's head. The first blow of the plastic stock did not calm the struggling soldier. Blancanales slammed him twice again before he went slack.

The Mexican commandos dragged the unconscious man off Lyons. The soldier, wearing green fatigues bearing the emblem of the International Group of the army of Mexico, wore a vest of Uzi mags and a canvas bag of fragmentation grenades. Blancanales appropriated the weapon and the bag of grenades. He pointed to the sound of the fighting.

Lyons nodded. "Teamwork. You pull, I throw."

Pulling safety pins, Blancanales passed the grenades to Lyons, who let the levers flip before he pitched the grenades into the lobby. He threw three grenades before anyone noticed the olive-green spheres bouncing over the carpet.

One fascist shouted, then a blast slammed him

against a wall. Blasts came fast and continuously as Lyons threw. He tossed all the eight grenades that the bag contained.

"Time to clean it up."

The North American and Mexican commandos rushed into the screams and swirling smoke. Wounded men and women raised pistols and shotguns. Others clawed the carpet to reach rifles. With an autoweapon in each hand, Blancanales killed everyone he saw, firing ambidextrous bursts from the M-16/M-203 and the Uzi.

Lyons kicked open the stairwell door. A bloody gunman pulled the pin from a grenade and swung back his arm. Lyons fired once, the point-blank blast tearing away the man's ribs and spinning him against the wall. Lyons closed the door. The steel fragments splintered the fire door with dozens of ragged holes.

A flash-shock boomed on the other side. The noise made Lyons stagger back. His body ached from the shock wave. Throwing the door open, he shouted, "*¡No más!* We are here! *¡Tenemos los fascistos! ¡Alto!*"

One soldier peered down. He saw Lyons and motioned to the others. A line of soldiers ran down the stairs. The lieutenant viewed the carnage in the elevator lobby. "Have you found the general?"

"No. But we only searched one office."

A fury of autofire broke out somewhere on the floor. The lieutenant shouted orders to his platoon. The young commandos went through the offices, searching methodically.

"There is still fighting below. My sergeant reports

a unit of federal agents attempted to come to the rescue of the fascists."

"Then we'll search through the building until we find him. Him and Gunther—"

"No, American. You must leave. This will be trouble to explain. It is impossible for you to stay."

"We won't go until we find Gunther and the general—"

Blancanales interrupted. "You heard him, Ironman. It's his country. We'll go now."

"It's our war! We got to track down all these Nazis and stomp them out."

"I thank you for your help," the Lieutenant repeated. "But now I must ask you to go."

Vato and the three Yaqui teenagers rushed around a corner. Their Mexican army uniforms splotched with blood, they reloaded their shotguns and rifles on the move. When they saw Lyons and Lieutenant Soto, they blinked as if in shock. Ixto collapsed against a wall, blood pouring from fragment slashes on his left arm. Jacom and Kino sat beside him. They tore off a dead man's shirt and used the shirt to make a compress. Vato joined Lyons and the Mexican officer.

"Have we cut off the head?" Lyons asked the Yaqui.

Vato pointed at the offices. "This head. But there are more. I know there must be more. This Trans-Americas *sociedad anónima* is everywhere. The offices have maps of all the countries. The war on my people in Sonora is only one of many."

"The lieutenant tells us to go—"

"I thank you for your courage," Lieutenant Soto

interrupted, "but this problem, this syndicate is Mexican. You have done what you can."

"Now it is a political problem." Vato nodded, agreeing with Lieutenant Soto.

"No!" Lyons countered. "It is criminal. These Nazis, the Communists, terrorists—they're only gangs of murderers. I refuse to call it political. It's not Mexican, it's not—"

"American," the lieutenant said, "it doesn't matter what you call it. It is what the *politicos* call it. But you and I know the truth. There is no disagreement between us. Now go. Take all your friends and go. The helicopter waits."

With a salute, Lieutenant Soto left the Yaqui and North Americans.

Lyons shouted to him, "But I'll come back! You understand?"

"Next time you come," the lieutenant answered, "call me first. It will prevent misunderstandings! Adios!"

Lyons and Vato gathered their partners. Minutes later, they flew from Mexico City in the captured troopship.

They had won a victory in Mexico.

But they had far from defeated the Fascist International.

IN AN INNER OFFICE OF THE SOVIET EMBASSY, Jon Gunther briefed the First Secretary on the attack against the International. Like Gunther, the First Secretary served the KGB.

"We lost most of those Mexicans, but it is not a

total disaster. One of the Americans wants our gold. He will sell himself to us.''

''Which one?''

''The blond one. I don't know his name. I will review our files.''

''Then why this massacre? If he—''

''He followed my instructions. He attempted to release me. But the other one, the Mexican criminal, he took me to his gang. The American followed instructions. I told him not to betray himself. And he did not. So he killed a few Mexicans? Now we have a man in the most secret of the American special units. I will contact him. I will pay him the gold I promised and much more. And in time, he will earn his money. Tonight was not a defeat. It was another step to victory....''

The True Adventures of Dick Stivers

Able Team author Dick Stivers has just returned from Colombo, Sri Lanka, and sends us this report:

What a beautiful country. How terrible and shameful this war.

My first week here I played tourist. I took the train from Colombo, a city on the tropical west coast, to Kandy, a city high in the mountains. I held on to the handrails at the steps into the cars and watched the landscape streak past. Waved at the farmers. Looked straight down into the canyons at orchards and rice paddies. Saw young women bathing in their sarongs, standing in mountain pools, pouring water over themselves, their glistening hair like night as it flowed over their shoulders.

I've been here a month now, interviewing people, taking hundreds of photos, listening to the official announcements. Some nights I lie awake and stare at the ceiling fan, thinking over what people have told me, comparing stories, cross-checking details: what streets looted and burned; how many families hacked to death, children burned alive, young men shot by the army or police, women mutilated; how many army trucks loading loot on what streets on what night.

For a week, the cities of Colombo, Kandy and Matale went insane. The Singhalese mobs did not attack the terrorists in the north who had murdered soldiers and policemen and government clerks. The mobs instead attacked decent people in the south whose only crime had been their ethnic background and enterprise and wealth.

In Matale, the Singhalese burned the buildings of the Tamil community: the Hindu temple, the stores, all the homes, the public-health centers. The only thing that stopped the Singhalese was time out to loot the stores. The Tamils escaped into the jungle. No one died there.

But in Colombo the mobs looted and burned entire streets. Police directed the mobs from one area to another. Officials in the government provided the leaders of the mobs with voter-registration lists. With the lists the leaders took their gangs from address to address in City of Colombo buses. The mobs divided the loot with the army and the army loaded their share onto trucks marked with government insignia. The police allowed the mobs to pass their guard posts. When Tamils and Muslims tried to defend their homes from the mobs, police and army units killed them with autoweapons and grenades.

Now the Singhalese pretend nothing happened. The politicians talk and talk and talk. The police and army pledge to stamp out Tamil terrorism. The newspapers denounce the lies of foreign journalists.

No one will ever know how many died. People have told me that the army and police took Tamil boys and no one else has seen them since. I have been informed that the authorities took truckloads of bodies out of the city— which the authorities have denied. I have heard rumors of bodies burned in graveyards.

In fact, I went out to find the body dumps. A Muslim taxi driver who spoke perfect Singhalese drove the car. With his light-colored skin and straight hair, he passes for a Singhalese. He helped me as revenge against the government; he lost relatives when a mob wiped out their shop, and he knows that the Muslims will be hit in the next "disturbances."

We drove the back roads around Colombo all day. Finally we found a Buddhist graveyard marked with tire tracks. Heavy vehicles had cut across the burial mounds. Tombstones and remembrance displays had been knocked down. We got out of the taxi and walked across the graveyard.

Near one side of the graveyard, pigs grunted and snorted as they fed on things sticking out of the soft dirt. A pig pushed around what looked like a white bowl. The outside of the bowl had hair on it.

A shattered skull.

The pigs cleaned ribs and scattered bones. As we watched, the pigs found a bone with blackened flesh on it. The pigs fought over the rotting meat.

I saw a pig uncover the remains of a small hand, perhaps a child's hand. I threw a rock at the pig and I took a step toward the hand. The dirt collapsed under my foot and I went in almost to my knee. The smell coming out of the hole drove me back.

Two Singhalese gravediggers walked over and watched us, so I made like a tourist. I picked up a skull and posed against a tombstone as the taxi driver took my picture. The skull had no jaw, and the pigs had broken away the palate and maxilla. The tissue-paper-thin bone of the skull makes me believe it came from someone old. The gravediggers laughed and joked as we left. The taxi driver told me they think tourists are crazy.

Now the Tamils and Muslims are preparing for the war. Everyone wants to learn karate. Some mornings I teach karate to Tamil and Muslim teenagers. I give them beginner lessons in killing with their hands and bricks and rocks, umbrellas and pipes. I bought rice sickles for one family. I tell people how to defend their street with gasoline and broken glass, how to defend against gasoline bombs.

Enough horror stories. Read the book when I write it.

Mack Bolan's

ABLE TEAM

by Dick Stivers

Action writhes in the reader's own street as Able Team's Carl "Mr. Ironman" Lyons, Pol Blancanales and Gadgets Schwarz make triple trouble in blazing war. To these superspecialists, justice is as sharp as a knife. Join the guys who began it all—Dick Stivers's Able Team!

"Able Team will go anywhere, do anything, in order to complete their mission. Plenty of action! Recommended!"

—*West Coast Review of Books*

#1 Tower of Terror
#2 The Hostaged Island
#3 Texas Showdown
#4 Amazon Slaughter
#5 Cairo Countdown
#6 Warlord of Azatlan
#7 Justice by Fire

#8 Army of Devils
#9 Kill School
#10 Royal Flush
#11 Five Rings of Fire
#12 Deathbites
#13 Scorched Earth
#14 Into the Maze

Able Team titles are available wherever paperbacks are sold.

GOLD EAGLE

You've not read action–adventure until you've read

Day of Mourning
Terminal Velocity
Dead Man Running

These are the three Mack Bolan books in which he began his incredible new career. No action-adventure reading is complete without this trilogy. Enjoy your greatest action experience ever in three linked stories that hurl the lethal human javelin known as The Executioner into the heart of world terror.

A wanton assault on Mack Bolan's command base leaves his one true love, April Rose, slain.

Fueled by white-hot rage and thoughts of wild revenge, The Executioner pursues his sacred quest to Moscow, lair of the sinister spearhead.

Bolan fingers the perpetrator in Russia and follows the trail of treachery back to the U.S. He rains a hellstorm of death on Washington, the city of lies, and comes face to face with the traitor at last—in the Oval Office itself!

"The best of the best." —*Florida Constitution*

HE'S UNSTOPPABLE. AND HE'LL FIGHT TO DEFEND FREEDOM!

Mail this coupon today!